THIRTY DAYS
HATH
SEPTEMBER

A NOVEL

Ronald Dwinnells

RIVER GROVE
BOOKS

Published by River Grove Books
Austin, TX
www.rivergrovebooks.com

Distributed by River Grove Books

Design and composition by Greenleaf Book Group and Sheila Parr
Cover design by Greenleaf Book Group and Sheila Parr
Cover images by ©Botond Horvath; ©Masson; ©Trif; ©stockyimages. Used under license from Shutterstock.com and Adobestock.com

Publisher's Cataloging-in-Publication data is available.

Print ISBN: 978-1-63299-817-0

eBook ISBN: 978-1-63299-818-7

First Edition

To my family—

Kathy, Erin, Sarah, Emily, Abbey, and Adam

Thirty days hath September,

April, June, and November.

All the rest have thirty-one,

Excepting February alone,

And that has twenty-eight days clear

And twenty-nine in each leap year.

1

First Lieutenant Delbert Vines was on his sixteenth bombing mission. Every muscle, big and small, was tense yet ready to react upon a sudden intentional or unconscious command. His heart sped like race cars around a speedway. He could even feel occasional skip beats as if those cars were tumbling off course.

Perspiration coated his skin, and his thick dark hair was damp underneath the headgear despite the high altitude's freezing temperatures, and worst of all, he constantly felt as if both his bladder and bowels would burst at a moment's notice.

Mesmerized by the constant barrage of flak surrounding his squadron's airspace, the bombardier couldn't halt his analytical mind from thinking that he only needed nine more sorties to get to his twenty-fifth. That magic number would get him a trip home. At least the rumor mill seemed to be consistent with that bit of gossip. He recently heard that the heavy bomber planes Hell's Angels and the Memphis Belle both completed their twenty-fifth mission earlier this year in May, and they got a break from this miserable war. The Belle even went home, and according to rumors, they're not coming back. So, there was hope!

Vines also knew about the other statistic that weighed heavily on everyone's mind. The one about how only half of the B-17 crew members never made it home. *They didn't become prisoners or end up in an enemy hospital with their wounds. They died! Half of us died for God's sake!* thought Vines.

My oh my, and what would Mildred do without me if I didn't come back? It was a little over a year ago when Cupid shot his arrows at the couple, and they instantly became soulmates. They were just right for each other. Perfect. Never an argument, disagreement, or even a scowl on their faces. Her melodic voice, the Victory roll hairstyle she wore, and her incredible warm blue-green eyes melted his soul—no matter how many times he looked at her. Mildred's smiles always gave him heart flutters while the scent of her skin and hair were like tropical paradise—so soothing. Even their embraces were like the classic hand-and-glove effect; they fit tightly and completely. They were meant for each other.

Everything always happened quickly these days. Meeting someone special, dating, falling in love, and even getting married moved at lightning speed as if life was in a big rush before it ended. The world was uncertain with all its violence and instability—so many unknowns.

Delbert Vines and Mildred Dixon talked about marriage exactly one week to the day of meeting each other. She accepted his proposal but wanted to wait until he came home. She wanted to make sure everything was done right and perfectly. Besides, she didn't want to get married and then receive a life-insurance settlement in case something awful was to happen.

"I don't want to marry your insurance policy, Delbert! I want to marry you because you are my truth, my always, and my forever!" Mildred said to him during their moments of intimacy.

Just then, a blinding explosion interrupted his musing. A dirty-gray wall of smoke spewed from both starboard engines and whooshed into the interior of the turbulent and vibrating B-17's fuselage. The blast veered the airplane off course, and it shifted from a steady forward movement to a wobbling motion.

A flurry of activities abruptly consumed the inside of the hollow metal tube as men and machines tumbled over and electrical sparks scattered helter-skelter, making it like a firework display at a Fourth of July celebration. The overwhelming thick smoke from the burning engines mixed with the strong metallic odor from the spurting and gushing blood of injured and dying crewmen made it difficult for the occupants to gasp for breaths.

Outside, the Luftwaffe's Messerschmitt Bf 109 fighters relentlessly attacked the heavier and slower US bombers that attempted to fly in formation. As the Bf 109s swarmed and attacked their victims like bees agitated by an intruder, some of the heavy planes faltered and fell from the sky.

Meanwhile, flak from numerous 88mm antiaircraft cannons stationed along the German countryside below exploded and released sharp metal fragments piercing the thin sheath of metal that protected men inside the B-17 aircraft.

Despite the furious chaos outside, made worse by the mind-altering explosions, a momentary calm, much like the eye of a hurricane, lulled the inside of the cabin. This was short-lived, however, as a noticeable descent pattern was soon detected, inciting panic for all those on board.

Vines hurtled backward, found himself just above the bomb bay area. The blast had propelled him and others through the air, bouncing one man after another off the steel interior frame and girder as if they were rubber balls at a racquetball court.

He was frigid, causing him to shake violently as the high-altitude chill seeped through every open pore of his damp skin. The damages that plagued the mechanical components failed to provide warmth to the interior.

He also found it increasingly difficult to inhale as he lay on the cold steel floor after being flung about. Suddenly, with an intense wave of claustrophobia incited by panic, the first lieutenant impulsively wanted to open the bomb bay hatches and jump toward the earth where he could be free of the oppressive violence. As hard as he tried, he could not move his legs and barely had control over his arms.

As visibility slightly improved after the first minutes of the explosion, Vines looked around the cabin, trying to adjust his eyes and focus his brain to the chaos and turmoil. He could barely make out the outline of two crewmen lying toward the aft, motionless. Too exhausted and hurt to crawl over to investigate, he assumed the worst.

The airman propped himself up against the inside skin of the fuselage wall but found it difficult to do so. His injured right arm was limp and nonresponsive. As he turned to inspect the injury, his eyes widened in horror. The arm was barely hanging by a single exposed strand of tendon from his shoulder. His Mae West life preserver had somehow slipped off, and blood soaked the shredded brown lambskin sleeves of his B-3 bomber jacket as fragments of bone embedded the outer tissues of skin and leather.

Vines, with his senses numbed and mind dulled from the pinball joggling that his body just went through, took inventory of his other injuries and thought how amazing it was that he felt no pain. His pain receptors were so overwhelmed that they could no longer function. Suddenly, with great clarity, he understood the impending catastrophe, whispered *damn* under his breath, and began to vomit all over himself.

As he wiped his mouth and nose with the sleeves of his jacket, a renewed sense of purpose seeped through his soul, and he reached into his left jacket pocket and slowly pulled out a folded sheet of paper kept in place with the hook of a pen.

Clicking the pen and unfolding two yellow sheets of legal paper with the help of his teeth, he started to scribble underneath, writing what he had previously started.

As Vines struggled to jot his thoughts, gushes of blood continued to pour out of his battered body, causing his consciousness to falter. Battling to stay alert, Vines made several more strokes on the wrinkled paper and then he was done. Despite the certain gloom and doom for his predicament, a faint smile formed across his face. He felt victorious in an impossibly winless situation that he had somehow overcome.

As the bombardier folded the note and hooked his pen around the edges, he noticed a movement on his left side from the cockpit area. Being delirious from a combination of hypothermia, injuries, blood loss, and difficulty breathing, Vines was unsure if he was hallucinating. He tried to focus on this movement. He was horrified to see a man resembling the B-17's copilot crawling toward him with an outstretched arm.

The man was dragging a sack that looked like a reserve parachute pack in his right hand. He did not utter a word as he kept making gestures for Vines to grab it.

Vines hesitated, not knowing if this was a dream or reality. *Am I going crazy? Is this a trick by an enemy who somehow snuck into the plane and is trying to lure me outside?*

Despite this, Vines shut his eyes tight for a moment. He needed to clear his mind. *The man cannot be real. The copilot must have died with that explosion! Who is he? Is the man really trying to help me?*

As he kept his eyes closed, the sounds began to slowly fade. The plane felt as if it was falling faster and at a steeper angle. At the same time, darkness seemed to be drawing near as if curtains were being drawn down over windows. He wanted so much to just relax his body and surrender to the blissful darkness of unconsciousness that was fighting so hard to win over him.

Yet, struggling between consciousness and oblivion, he knew he didn't have much time left to act if he were to survive. The plane was plunging faster, steeper, and sharper with every passing second.

Abruptly from somewhere—the recesses of his mind or, perhaps, the voice of God or even an angel—he heard a soft but intense feminine voice. Vines looked around, instantly recognizing the voice belonged to Mildred. He could even smell her! In his confused state, he called out, "Mildred? Mildred? Why are you here? Where are you, my sweet love?"

The voice then whispered, "Clear your mind, Delbert! Jump! You must jump! Grab the chute and jump. Save yourself!"

Frightened, yet comforted at the same time, he wondered, *Where is this coming from?* Balancing between a state of delirium and reality, he was confused and afraid. He took a few deep breaths—clearing his mind and trying to make sense of what was happening to him. Then, with renewed determination and a sense of calm and peace that eased his soul, First Lieutenant Delbert Vines pulled himself up and feebly grabbed the sack from the man.

2

The light breeze drifting through the open window gently brushed against her face and fluffed her wispy white hair. A hint of the air's crisp early autumn scent put a smile on Mildred Dixon's face. It was a welcome relief during the hot, sultry September morning.

Catching a glimpse of herself in a window reflection, as she scanned the room, Mildred stopped to study her face. The night-light was angled perfectly to reveal a full reflection of her face. There seemed to be more creases than yesterday, she observed. Some were deep while others were barely perceptible as they etched and carved interesting lines upon the woman's aging face. She then turned her head and squinted to glance at the Big Ben alarm clock. Unlike the breeze, the morning light had not yet peeked through the bedroom window, permitting the luminous dials to glow brightly in the early dawn. The time glared 4:59 a.m.

Mildred woke up with a hangover—again! Just like every morning, her face was puffy, her eyes were swollen, and she had a gnawing headache that just wouldn't go away. It consumed her very being. It wasn't that she habitually drank or even took medications. Going to bed late, waking up a couple of times to pee, and thinking about the same things over and over, night after night, made it difficult to sleep. Then, most mornings, she felt as if she was clobbered by a Mack truck with heavy gravel in its bed.

Ever since she got that notice from a Western Union telegram that Delbert was missing in action—almost forty years ago—sleep evaded her; she had never experienced a full eight hours of rest without interruptions, not even for two hours at a time. Last night was especially difficult. Between the discomfort of the heat—despite two oscillating fans at full speed—and the thoughts of her impending trip to the hospital in the morning, restful sleep evaded her once again.

Everything seemed business as usual until a visit to her family doctor, two days ago, that prompted a medical referral. Mildred had not felt well—just not herself—for a few weeks. "I have no energy," she told friends. She tired often and quickly, especially when her belly pain acted up. Sometimes the pain—stabbing pain—was so intense it shot straight to her back.

Mildred's appetite fluctuated, too. She had very little interest in eating, the effects of which showed as her clothes began hanging on her.

Her doctor explained that she needed admission to the A. B. Chandler Medical Center in Lexington. He would not tell her what was wrong or what his concerns were. The doctor poked and prodded Mildred's belly for a long while and asked terse but specific questions about her weight changes and bowel habits. He even sent Mildred for some blood tests and an X-ray at the local hospital. The next day, he called and explained that she needed more tests—this time at the "big" medical center in Lexington.

"It's a hospital run by the University of Kentucky and the best around this area.

It's a regional referral center, and they have a lot of smart people and experts who can figure out complex medical problems. They'll be able to help you, Mildred. I want to get you there as soon as possible—just for some tests for now. I don't think it's anything bad; we just need to make sure you're okay. You'll be home in a couple of days so you can tend to that gorgeous garden of yours."

Trying to ease her worries a bit, the doctor said, "You know that we've been friends for a long time, and you're my main supplier of those giant watermelons! And I love the turnips we dig up in the fall, too! So fun to dig 'em up and just plain delicious! I can hardly wait to sauté 'em in lots of butter, garlic, and salt! Real good, Mildred! Heaven on earth for sure!"

As her thoughts were preoccupied with her troubles and apprehension loomed, she slowly arose from the soft goose-down bedding and maintained a sitting position for a moment. Her low blood pressure always acted up when she got out of bed, so she learned to always get up slowly.

With legs dangling off to one side, she took inventory of her bedroom as she did every morning. Her blue-green eyes, already adjusting to the early dawn light, scanned the room as deftly as a pro quarterback would a football field, knowing where every player on both sides was at every moment. As always, her eyes settled upon the black-and-white photo and the framed portrait sketch that sat on her bedside dresser. A necklace with a plain ring dangling from it sat next to the portrait.

The image on the right was a sketch of a man's face, done in charcoal. He had a kindly face and a grin that brought sparkles not only to his eyes but to his entire well-chiseled face, too. His features were strong, contrasting sharply with the gentleness of his eyes. A 1940s military hat sat slightly angled atop his thick crop of dark hair. The collar of a bomber jacket was partially visible resting on his neck.

The adjacent photo, framed in a beautiful, scrolled gold, showed two people walking side by side with the background slightly blurred and even a little faded. The man with the same face as the sketch appeared to be laughing.

The woman stood about half a foot shorter and appeared to be in her early twenties, sporting light shoulder-length hair adorned with soft flowing waves. The hairstyle, she remembered, was pretty much the same on most women. It was called the Victory roll, which showed off a lot of curls and gave them a full-body look. Both wore military uniforms common during World War II. She was gazing at the man as if no others existed. It was no ordinary stare but a look of deep love, caring, and happiness. Her broad smile made her cheeks so prominent that her eyes could barely be seen.

After a moment of studying the images, Mildred closed her eyes as if remembering and perhaps reliving that moment in time. Opening her eyes after a few seconds, she grasped the necklace and placed it around her neck, as she did every morning, holding the ring tightly.

A pleasant smile slowly emerged from her face, and after a few seconds, she gently placed both feet into her waiting slippers. Shuffling toward the bathroom to prepare for the day's ordeal, a perfectly formed teardrop rolled slowly onto her left cheek and down her neck until it was halted by the fabric of her soft cotton gown. She sniffled once, then began to prepare for the challenging day ahead.

3

There were no cars approaching the frenzied outer lane of the busy high-way, so the Yellow Cab driver shifted the 1941 Plymouth sedan to first gear while letting up on the clutch. He simultaneously depressed his right foot against the accelerator pedal. The two female passengers had just gotten in and settled into the spacious back seat when a loud bang against the front passenger window suddenly caught his attention.

He abruptly halted and reached over to roll down the window. "This cab's taken, buddy!"

The skinny red-headed man in a khaki military uniform said, "We need to get over to Broadway as soon as possible. Can you just squeeze us in? Are these ladies going near there and can we jump in?"

"They're going to West Broadway and Fourth, but it's up to them if they wanna share the ride!"

Twenty-three-year-old Mildred Dixon and her best friend, Helen Hicks, were on their way to see friends at a rooftop garden party at the Brown Hotel. They were adorned with makeup that took over an hour to apply and dressed in party dresses, so they were anxious to get there without any unforeseen interruptions. They were already late, and

Helen, annoyed and perturbed by the intrusion said, "Just go, cabby, those boys can find their own ride."

Mildred intervened. "No, Helen, they are nice and one's a dreamboat. The uniforms are nice, too—so clean and crisp. Men are always so handsome in uniforms, don't you think? You know in a few months they'll be risking their lives for us on the battlefield. We need to do our part, Helen. Let's help them out." She then directed her reply to the driver, smiled at the two men standing outside of the cab, and said, "Yes, we are okay with the boys riding with us, but please take us to our destination first."

"You got it, ladies! Get in, fellas!"

The tall man with a nice smile slid into the front passenger side, took off his hat, looked and nodded to Mildred, and said, "Thank you, ma'am." The red-headed man began to talk gibberish as he got into the back seat. He then wedged himself in between the two women, smiled at them both, and continued his nebulous nattering.

Abruptly, he stopped and turned his head either way and said, "Wowser, bowser! Holy mackerel, you dames . . . er . . . I mean you ladies are gorgeous." Looking at Helen, he said, "Name's Van. Van Miller. You're a real cookie! What's a fella got to do to spend the rest of his life with you?"

"Dream a lot," Helen shot back. "Look, you're a cheesy guy and probably a drip, okay. So, keep your mouth shut, your hands to yourself, mind your manners, and when we get off, you can drool all over yourself, but for now, keep your gobbledygook to yourself! We want to keep our dresses clean and neat and not have your slime all over us."

Mildred kept quiet, eyeing the man riding shotgun next to the driver. She couldn't see his name tag and didn't find a good opening to start a conversation. He was the most beautiful man she'd ever laid eyes on. His thick, wavy black hair perfectly sat atop his deeply set eyes, perfectly angled jawline, and prominent chin. He had the prettiest blue eyes she'd ever seen. Not a brilliant blue, but a dullish shade that appeared almost translucent. She couldn't help thinking that his eye color resembled a blue sky surrounded by magenta clouds. She'd seen the color before, especially during sunsets, when the light hit that blue patch at just the right angle, creating a rich pastel blue just as the sun faded away over the horizon. His body language revealed a relaxed poise and a great deal of self-confidence.

Mildred was surprised by her whimsical thoughts. She knew in an instant that this was the man she had been waiting for her entire short life. Out of nowhere, he had appeared—like a thick fog had suddenly lifted, and everything was revealed. She could see her future clearly and visibly. For a second, she even fancied herself donning a wedding gown. *My heavens. What's gotten into you, Mildred? How capricious can you be?* she thought.

Mildred had fallen in love with a man she knew nothing about. No name—at least not yet. No exchange of words and no idea if he was a good man or a bad one—she just knew he was for her.

But why? How could this happen? She wanted to talk with him but didn't dare at this moment while Helen and the smiley red-haired man were having a comical fight.

"West Broadway and Fourth. The Brown Hotel!" the taxi driver yelled as he was slowing down. "Ladies, you need to get out right away—the traffic is backed up, and I don't want to get stuck here!"

After the car turned right onto Fourth Street from Broadway, it came to a stop. Mildred jumped out onto the sidewalk and Helen quickly climbed over the talkative man named Miller, according to his nameplate on his uniform, and onto the sidewalk next to Mildred. She turned around and announced to the cab driver, "These boys will take care of the fare, won't you, boys?"

"But, Helen, you—"

Mildred had the money to hand over, but Helen pushed it aside, grabbed her by the elbows, and proceeded into the hotel entrance as fast as she could go. The dark-haired man started laughing while Van Miller began to curse at the women.

The cab driver then asked, "So where you gents headed to now?" Miller, a bit stunned and stymied by what just transpired said, "I think this place might be where we're headed. Is the Brown Hotel the same place as the Brown?"

"Yup, boys!" Then in a sarcastic tone, he added, "Just like the

United States is the same as the States, and they sometimes call me a cabby, but I'm called a cab driver, too. All the same . . . yup the Brown Hotel is the Brown all right!" The driver shook his head in some disgust. "Looks like you meatheads got had by a couple of con women. Pay up, or I don't let you out! Make it darn fast, boys! I got traffic behind me. Funniest damn thing I've seen happen to a couple of fat heads in a while!" he said, chuckling.

4

The overhead page blared loudly: "Jack Maizel, report to Six North, STAT! Mr. Maizel to Six North, STAT!"

The fourth-year medical student barely heard his name when the automatic glass doors of the front entranceway slid open. Though it was already warm and humid outside, the fresh air felt good against his face. Reflexively, he shaded his tired eyes and squinted from the brilliant sunlight beaming over the early morning horizon. He spotted a lone jet directly above spewing a long, thin contrail against the clear blue sky.

Pausing for a few seconds before stepping out, he swiped his hand down his face, stroked his two-day stubble, and raked back his long, unwashed, greasy hair.

Damn! Won't these people just leave me the hell alone? Damn! Why are they calling me right now? Right now, just as soon as I left the maternity ward! Don't they know I've been stuck in this place for two straight days?

It was a horrific night to be on call for the OB-GYN floor. He was awake most of the night, starting IVs on newly admitted pregnant women and checking cervical dilations every few minutes on every patient who was in active labor. Jack Maizel even assisted on two deliveries—one of them a long and complicated Cesarian section due to the baby failing to progress along the birth canal.

The incessant screams of women in labor exhausted Jack. It gave him such anxiety that memories of himself as a twelve-year-old boy tending to his injured and beloved horse after a riding accident always crept back into his memory.

He and Ajax had just won a local two-day dressage event when an accident badly shattered her right hind leg, resulting in euthanasia. "Destroy her right away!" said Jack's mother to one of her horse trainers. He felt so helpless as two burly men picked him up and took him away while his mother did the unthinkable deed. In the years ahead, Jack would never escape the feelings of sadness and regret that he could not save his best friend's life.

Now, he was tired and just wanted to go to his apartment to sleep for a couple of hours and do something he wanted to do—like getting a round of golf in.

After a few seconds of contemplating whether he should respond to the overhead page or simply ignore it, Jack shrugged, slung the heavy backpack over his right side, and hurriedly walked away from the building.

"Damn!" he whispered to himself.

"Jack!" A loud voice boomed somewhere not far behind the crowd of people exiting the building. Most had just finished their shift and wanted to get home or run a few errands before they napped off the previous evening. "Where are you going, Jack? Did you not hear that stat page? Dr. Jones would like your presence on the medicine floor, pronto!"

Jack pretended not to hear the familiar voice of his Tanzanian-born friend. He always loved listening to the unique accent, a mix of East African and British—a result of early childhood influence from a local British missionary school. For now, he completely ignored the warning as he quickened his pace. *Damn! Damn! Damn! These people just don't get it! Leave me the hell alone! Just leave me alone! Please!*

The man got farther behind in the crowd, but because he was so tall, he could keep track of his prey. "Excuse me, please, Jack Maizel! I beg of you—no—I sincerely ask you to please come back. They want you up there right now! We have been waiting quite some time! It is most imperative that you are present!"

Walk faster, Jack! Come on! I gotta get out of here!

"Sir! My friend!" The musical voice, now even louder said, "What, may I ask, is the matter with you? Did you not hear me? Dr. Jones wants you to be present for rounds! Now! Please do not agitate him. Remember, he is our boss this month. The chairman of the department, Jack! He will be resoundingly upset if you are absent on the first day of our new rotation! You are already missing the morning rounds!"

Jack, half a foot shorter than the African man and carrying a bit too much weight as a result of his indulgence in fast foods, was a bit winded as he trotted across the street. He turned his head slightly and yelled back, "Cover for me, Ahgri! I'll catch you at the golf course at ten sharp! Be there, buddy!"

"Jack!" Ahgri Zuri shouted out one last time. Realizing his friend was gone and was not going to heed him, he spoke lightly—more to himself than Jack, "You cannot just leave! Do not be mischievous! It will not end well for you, my friend!"

Ahgri, a classmate of Jack's, was frustrated. He now stopped giving chase and just stood there deflated while watching his friend cross the street and disappear between buildings. He never understood his friend. Jack was so smart, grasping complicated medical concepts, but he was a sour human being with no sense of responsibility and didn't seem to care about anything or anyone. Ahgri just shook his head, and with a deep sigh re-entered the building, and loudly declared to no one in particular, "You are a *pumbaa*, Jack Maizel! Nothing but a no-good *pumbaa*!"

5

Two physically mismatched men, one tall and thin and the other shorter and slightly overweight, stood at the perimeter of the putting green. Ahgri Zuri was impeccably dressed in a green, red, and yellow wide-striped Polo shirt matching his freshly pressed lime-green golf slacks. He stood tall, six feet seven, in shiny brown alligator golf shoes that matched his belt. His thick locs gave him a distinguished appearance. He loved getting dressed up. It gave him confidence and pride in his Tanzanian heritage.

Jack Maizel, Ahgri's best friend in medical school, was shirtless and wore an overused and out-of-shape baseball cap strapped tightly around his disheveled greasy hair, its bill sticking backward. Cutoff jeans and sneakers without the benefit of socks completed his unappealing dress. It certainly violated the golf club's dress code, but he couldn't care less about those rules.

Ahgri was often disgusted with Jack's lack of hygiene and his choice of wardrobe.

Always the feisty of the two, Jack often bragged and feigned pride to be known as the only person to get kicked off at most of the golf course clubs in and around Lexington—at least twice each. The manner of his dress and a sometimes combative nature with other golfers were his primary downfall. He'd even managed to be *forever* banned from all but two of the local clubs. If it weren't for his parents' wealth, they would likely never have invited him back again!

"You're gonna miss that hole, Zuri, so you might as well quit now!"

"Uh-huh," was all Ahgri uttered as he gently swayed his putter back in a small arc, then lightly tapped the fluorescent orange golf ball toward the hole about four feet away. It moved slowly at first but gained momentum as the ball rolled down a slight slope toward the hole. Suddenly the ball disappeared into the eighteenth hole as if something swallowed it.

"Shit!" the shirtless man exclaimed. "I just don't get it! People as tall as you aren't supposed to be able to play golf, especially you native Africans!"

Ahgri, unperturbed, kept a calm but stern demeanor. Acting much like a stuffy university professor with a slight hint of self-importance, Jack's classmate for the past three years, retorted, "When people resort to humor based on skin color, ethnicity, or even someone's poor command of the language, it typically means that the offender is afraid of something and possesses poor self-esteem. You, Jack Maizel, may hail from a rich family and perhaps you are smarter than me—although that certainly is debatable—but it does not mean that you are superior to me in terms of kindness, generosity, empathy, experience, athleticism, and, most importantly, the fullness of life!"

Slumping his posture slightly, and a bit embarrassed, Jack felt as if he were melting much like the Wicked Witch of the West in *The Wizard of Oz*! *I need to get on the offensive*, he thought.

Ahgri appeared even more erect as he locked eyes with Jack and ended his soliloquy by stating, "Yes, I firmly believe you are afraid, and I believe that you fear *me*! Immensely! So, either refrain from using that type of language or cease your presence around me. I shall not tolerate it! Also, please quit refusing to pay me the twenty dollars you now owe me, Jack. You and your arrogant richness gambled that you were superior to me by wagering against me in a simple game of golf. As quoted by many wise men, a bet is a bet. Simply put, I won, and you lost, my friend!" Staying calm but with a stern demeanor and arms now akimbo, Ahgri Zuri said, "In my country, we call people like you *pumbaa*! In fact, many white people are known as *pumbaa* there. They are just not very smart. Like you! So, just pay up, like a gentleman should. Be honorable and respectful!"

Jack shot back, "How mixed up is that? You're an African native guy impersonating a Caribbean dude but trying to act like an American black man! That's weird, bro! Mark my word, there are no gentlemen where you come from, Zuri!"

Ahgri Zuri, being as refined and well-mannered as he could, said, "Jack, I will not stoop to your level. I am a better man than that. Please do not say anything further. You will only embarrass yourself." As his friend continued, the sophisticated and gentlemanly Ahgri stayed calm and looked the other way, shaking his head sideways in a gesture of dismay.

Ignoring Ahgri's statements, Jack Maizel continued trying to annoy his friend with his next barb: "Golf is a highly skillful game for highly sophisticated people!"

Ahgri knew that his friend was trying to use psychology to avoid paying the twenty-dollar debt from the bet. He was trying to get into Ahgri's head through contempt, but it wasn't working as far as the African man was concerned. *What a poor sport he is*, thought Ahgri. He was getting tired of Jack and was anxious to get back to the medical center.

"Look, Jack, please quit harassing me! You're up to your no-good tactics again. You just think I am going to forget about the twenty dollars you owe me by getting me upset. It will not work. I'm not forgetting, so pay up. Please! Anyway, we need to get back to the hospital. You already skipped this morning's rounds. Dr. Jones asked me to go look for you this morning. When I returned without you, he was angry and took it out on me. I will not be yelled at again because of your irresponsibility. Do you understand me, Jack?"

The shirtless man ignored him.

"Jones is an ass," said Jack. He handed Ahgri a twenty. "You're one tough SOB, mountain man. Come on, let's do another round!"

"No way, Jack. Did you not hear me? We need to get back for Dr. Jones's lecture. He will be very disappointed in us both if we are not there!"

Jack snorted. "Why are you so worried about getting in trouble? That should be normal for guys like you. How many times have you been in jail, Zuri? I heard they put folks in jail all the time in Tanzania! Right?"

Ahgri remained stoic and stone-faced.

"So, relax, don't worry about this guy! He's so damn old he doesn't know who the hell any of us are. I bet he thinks we're brothers!" Jack laughed. "Anyway, I'm not interested in that internal medicine stuff. Plastic surgery's my game. That's where the money's at, ace. If you want to be rich, you'll go into surgery with me. That's what my dad says, and he's pushing me to do just that! You know, do a couple of boob jobs, lift some asses, and smooth out some lines on old rich women and you got yourself a nice Benz or a Porsche in a couple of days, man! You can make a few thousand bucks with these simple procedures. Do a bunch of 'em, and you'll have that ragtop paid up in a single day. That primary medical care stuff is for the birds. My folks are rich, and I'm going to make damned sure I stay that way, too. I'm not going to be no lowly primary care doc—you know let's do it for humanity's sake, right? If you do that for a living, you'll be driving some cheap ol' Ford junker all your life. My dad always said you can't have too much money!"

The impeccably dressed and distinguished Ahgri looked at his friend dumbfoundedly and simply replied, "In my country, people would call you *punda bubu*! Dumbass. You know that you will never become a surgeon. It is not in your spiritual being, my friend. You are intrigued by people who are without means. We discussed this many times. By helping them, you help yourself because it makes you feel good. You want to help those who are helpless. I know this with all my heart! You once told me about your horse, Ajax, and how she got injured. You tried to care for her without telling anyone because you knew they would terminate her life if they found out about the accident. You had so much compassion, Jack! Don't let that go, my friend! You have a good soul and your destiny is to help the downtrodden, the helpless, and the needy. I know you, Jack! Follow your heart and not your rich parents' wishes for their own secondary gain. So come on, Jack, let's go. Let's go and learn how we can become good doctors, please!"

The shirtless man knew his friend was right, but he was upset at being called a dumbass again. One of the first Swahili words Ahgri Zuri used to describe him. Jack looked down, inhaled deeply, and made no reply. He simply picked up his golf bag and started walking away from the clubhouse and toward the first hole.

"Jack! What are you doing? Where are you going? What is wrong with you? Did you not hear anything I said? Dr. Jones will have your hide if you don't attend the lecture!"

The medical student stopped dead in his tracks and turned around.

"Look, Zuri, Dr. Tenneson is on the front nine. I saw him there! You heard of him, right? Dr. John Tenneson? The biggest name in plastic surgery in Kentucky. My dad knows him, and he told me that I need to own his practice someday. He told me I should hang out with him every chance I get. So, I'm just going to see if I can catch up with Dr. God and score some points. The hell with Jones!"

He then turned and sauntered away, leaving his friend.

Once again, Ahgri shook his head in disgust, breathed the words *punda bubu*, and walked the other way.

6

Jack was thrilled. He just competed through the half pirouette in the walk, trot half pass, and canter half pass for the fourth level of the dressage competition. The three-day event included a cross-country and a show jump phase so the horses could demonstrate their excellent conditioning and superior maneuverability. Ajax was amazing—as usual. She nailed the pirouette as if she'd been doing it all her life! So many hours of training, usually every day and well into darkness before the boy and his horse called it a day. She did her maneuvers so perfectly.

Jack just received his final score card from one of the judges, and they did well. Mostly 10s. They should get first place in their division, he thought.

The horse and the boy made their way to the open lawn toward the sprawling oak tree just beyond the perimeter of the grandstand. Jack wanted to rest Ajax under the coolness of the shade. The competition was winding down, but they could still hear the crowd gasp—oohs and aahs—as the horses made their incredible and delicate movements. As a light breeze passed by under the tree, Jack was undoing the meticulous braids on Ajax's mane that he spent several hours braiding just two days before to prepare for the competition. He was reflecting on how he and Ajax got to this level of competition.

As an only child, Jack had thought of the Appaloosa as his best friend and constant companion since his fifth birthday, when his father brought the foal home on a horse trailer.

Jack's mother was so angry with her husband for that. How dare he mess up her farm with a "mutant," as she called the Appaloosa. She demanded to know what came across his mind by giving their son a non-Thoroughbred horse to live on her pure Thoroughbred racehorse farm. Had he lost all his marbles? "This isn't America, the land of the melting pot! It's Kentucky, the land of the pure! We live in Thoroughbred country! But now we must live on a tainted horse farm where everyone will turn their heads twice to get a sight of the spotted Appaloosa running around in our fields that is reserved exclusively for our Thoroughbreds! I am so embarrassed! I should just go on out there and shoot that hideous thing!"

Jack loved Ajax. They became childhood best friends. He shared his dreams and fantasies and even hurtful times when his mother would yell at him. The Appaloosa was always true to Jack, listening patiently, snorting, grunting, or whinnying to acknowledge he was attentive and was there for him. They had grown so close that Jack knew he wanted more than anything to be the protector of all animals when he grew up. He wanted to be an animal rights activist and operate an animal sanctuary for any animals, but especially horses, so he could always be with Ajax as he got older.

When Jack looked up, an overweight man, donning an oversize bowler hat, had sauntered toward Jack and Ajax as they were cooling down. The portly man stood staring for a few minutes with his thumbs hooked around his suspenders that framed an ill-fit and wrinkled suit. Clearing his throat, he said, "Pardon me, laddie, my name is Smythe! Colonel Garland Smythe, formerly of Her Majesty's Armed Forces." He suddenly straightened his stance with his double chin jutting out and raised a bit high. "That horse resembles the cartoon version of the *One Hundred and One Dalmatians*! What do you call him, Pongo?" He roared, laughing as his chin, which resembled a turkey's wattle, quivered while he shot out small missiles of spittle from his mouth. His face became flushed, and the laughter soon turned into a coughing jag. After about a minute of this display that included choking, Colonel Smythe said, "And who are you supposed to be, the boy version of Cruella de Vil?" He laughed again and coughed some more.

Jack was terrified of the man. He wasn't sure what he could do to get away from him.

"Look, lad, I do not mean to laugh, but you offer me a spectacle truly worthy of humor. An Appaloosa breed at a dressage event . . . with a wee laddie nevertheless!" He laughed a third time. "Well, let me tell you one thing, Appaloosas are not built to do these dressage events. What you need is a Dutch Warmblood or even better a German Westphalian! The West can jump like a Mexican jumping bean! They are the best for these types of competitions." He looked at Ajax, amusingly and said, "Not a Dalmatian!" He snorted this time, trying to contain his outbursts.

"Look, mister," said Jack, standing up to the man, "Ajax is a mare, and she's the best. I got her on my fifth birthday when she was just a filly. She was one then."

"And, how old would you be now, laddie?"

With arms akimbo, Jack said, "I just turned twelve a few months ago!"

With an expression of surprise, the man said, "Twelve! You are twelve years old. I apologize! You are not a lad at all. You are a bloody tot!" This time, Smythe could not contain another outburst of laughter complete with the coughing, choking, and, this time, excessive tearing.

After he finally calmed down, he said, "You are too young for such a mature sport as dressage. You have the wrong breed of horse, and you are simply not suited for this event. You must be older and more experienced to become a champion. How old is the Dalmatian? Seven, I suspect?" Without waiting for a response, he continued, "So, my young lad, your horse performed well today—I was surprised you did that well, but get a professional trainer if you are serious about this; otherwise cease wasting everyone's time and your father's money!"

Just then, Jack's mom approached.

"Jack, get on that horse and take her for a ride!"

She then directed her attention to the man and aggressively addressed him, "Do you know who I am, sir?"

He looked a bit intimidated and said, "Yes, of course, Miss Burk. Everyone knows who you are, madam."

She pointed her index finger up near his face. "Well, you are wrong there. I am Mrs. Burk-Maizel, and that is my son, Jack. I heard you harassing him, and I don't like it. You will apologize when he comes back from that ride. Then after that, I don't ever want to see hide or hair of you at any horse events in this part of the country. Do I make myself clear, sir?"

As the man was building up his courage for his response, a sudden loud thud followed by a short scream sounded from a distance, interrupting the conversation. A crowd quickly formed as people ran toward a recumbent horse and the boy kneeling beside her. The horse thrashed her head, whinnying and snorting loudly. The boy stroked the horse's neck and talked to her, tears in his eyes but not crying out.

"Jack, are you okay?" Jack didn't hear his mother's question as she rushed to him. He was too focused on Ajax to respond.

Just then someone in the crowd said, "That horse's right forelimb is broke. Look, you can see it's twisted!"

Jack's mother could see right away the leg was fractured. "The horse needs to be destroyed. Right now!" someone in the crowd yelled out. His mother nodded exuberantly, as if she wanted to act right away.

Jack was experiencing a living nightmare. Feeling helpless, he could not believe what he heard and witnessed from his mother. He fought back from bursting out and kept his tears at bay. He said, "No, she's not sick. She just has a small injury. She'll be okay!"

Jack's mother said, "Jack, you walk back to the truck and the trailer hitch right now. And don't you look back this way. Now, go!"

Jack could not believe it. She was going to kill Ajax! "They can fix her leg; I know they can! You don't have to kill her! Don't kill Ajax, Mom! Please . . ."

"Now go, Jack, or I will drag you there myself. Someone, get this boy over to my truck and do it damn quick. I will take care of this situation," she said, pulling a Glock from her purse.

Jack's eyes widened. He was on the verge of hysteria now.

Smythe suddenly appeared, panting, but approached Jack and took him by his hand. He then directed his attention to Jack's mother. "Mrs. Burk-Maizel, I must say, destroying this horse without a proper examination by a veterinarian may be a premature decision and somewhat drastic. Why not wait a short time, until a veterinarian can assess this horse?"

"She needs to be put out of her misery! Besides, I told you to beat it already. Mind your own business," Jack's mother said, a slight smirk on her face as she looked back at the Appaloosa.

The colonel gazed at her for a moment, shaking his head slightly as if he couldn't believe this woman was going to take action on this poor horse and this lad. He then gently took Jack's hand and said, "Come on, lad. Let's walk back to your mother's truck. It is something that cannot be helped."

Jack, sobbing, pulled away and threw himself onto Ajax's body, grasping at the mane he had just unbraided. Two men rushed over and roughly grabbed Jack by the arms, picked him up, and headed toward the truck. Jack tried to lash out at them with all his might, bawling and screaming and saying he wouldn't leave Ajax, but the men were too strong.

A few minutes later, Jack heard a single gun blast. He stopped crying.

7

The gold embroidered name and title over his left breast pocket affirmed the important position he held: *William D. Jones, MD, PhD, Internal Medicine Chairman.* It conveyed professionalism and dignity. The lightly starched white clinician's coat was impeccably tailored and pressed. With the black tubing of a stethoscope folded and stashed in the right lower pocket, the man offered quite a distinct presentation.

Some saw Dr. Jones as a haughty man, while others admired him for his silver-screen good looks and a demeanor that commanded respect. Walking with purposeful determination, he made eye contact with everyone who walked by, nodding to some and cordially greeting others. His graying hair, perfectly coifed, and chiseled facial features gave him an appearance of wisdom and excellence. The man's expensive cologne even made him smell important.

In sharp contrast was Jack Maizel. Dr. Jones approached the sloppy-looking student just outside of the internal medicine administrative offices and said, "Mr. Maizel, follow me to my office! Now!"

Jack's hair was greasy and slightly tousled, and Dr. Jones could see an impression around the student's forehead formed by a tightly fitted ball cap. He looked like a karate expert wearing a hachimaki.

The student followed the imposing attending physician.

Jack, wearing a pair of wrinkled khakis with an equally wrinkled and misbuttoned shirt, entered the physician's office. He immediately went for the luxurious leather chair that sat in front of Dr. Jones's large oak desk.

"Don't sit, Mr. Maizel, you won't have time," said Dr. Jones.

Dr. Jones's steely blue eyes peered over his reading glasses, making eye contact with Jack. His militaristic tone harkened back to his tour of duty during the Vietnam War. He had been commander of a battlefield hospital and adhered to the strictest codes that dictated service, discipline, and order. He had very little tolerance for irresponsibility and lack of focus on duty. Dr. Jones always maintained this demeanor of strictness and impeccability, hoping that this characteristic would carry over to his students.

"I noticed you were neither at morning rounds nor my noon lecture today. Not a good way to start your rotation in internal medicine, would you agree?" He continued without waiting for a response. "Do you understand cause and effect, Mr. Maizel? Do you know when there are expectations and you fail to meet them, consequences will soon follow? Those consequences tend to *not* be favorable, especially if there is insubordination and no capacity to follow rules. It appears you fit into that category. It that correct?"

Dr. Jones gave Jack a cold stare as he spoke, but Jack did not respond. Either this student was just too dumb to comprehend or he was being obstinate and simply displaying a classic passive-aggressive tactic. He didn't care either way.

"Have you ever heard of responsibility? Is it even in your lexicon, Mr. Maizel?" Again, without waiting for a response, Dr. Jones pressed on. "This is quite disturbing to me, especially when you have signed up for the acting intern position on my service. As you may know or at least have heard, this is a tremendously important position and only the most talented and responsible students may take this on. I am a bit uncertain how you got on my service, Mr. Maizel!" Dr. Jones paused for effect. "I would like to add that this is your first day with me. I'm certain you have a good explanation for your behavior and your actions, or should I say inaction, to not attend to your assigned tasks. I am not interested in your excuses, so don't give me any!

"Since you were not good enough to show up for my lecture today, I am assigning you to be on call tonight and the next three consecutive nights. You will pick up all new patients that come in this afternoon at four and you will work them up completely with a detailed report on the history and physical exam at morning rounds tomorrow and the ensuing mornings. If you have forgotten, the morning rounds start promptly at seven, Mr. Maizel. I expect an eloquent presentation on each new patient, complete with differential diagnoses of each problem and a detailed set of action plans. I also expect you to understand the complete pathophysiology of each medical condition."

Dr. Jones's voice became louder as he continued with his monologue. "I'm sure you don't have any questions or comments, so you are now dismissed." With that, the doctor focused his gaze on a document on his desk and began reviewing it.

The silence was agonizing. Jack stood there shocked, incomprehension written across his face. He could not move for a few seconds and had become almost catatonic.

After a few seconds, Dr. Jones looked up and over his glasses. "Must I repeat myself? You are excused, *Mr.* Maizel! Please remove yourself from my presence. Sooner rather than later!"

"But, Dr. Jones, I have a dinner engagement tonight with my father and Dr. Tenneson. You know who he is, right? He's the most important plastic surgeon in Lexington and—"

"Mr. Maizel! You may be a bright student and you may not have to attend my lectures to do well and graduate with your doctorate's degree, but as long as I am the attending physician for my service this month, I will be the one who gives you your grades and orders. That means you will do exactly as I command or risk failing and repeating the rotation. Perhaps you don't care, but I will make it my mission to have you not graduate from this medical school unless you shape up, sir! In my opinion, you are not ready to take on the role of *doctor*! So, I suggest you do a considerable amount of introspection—soul-searching, if you will—and grow up a little bit! Also, might I remind you, you are doing an internal medicine clerkship during the entire month of September—not surgery or anything else." Dr. Jones paused for a moment. "And most certainly not plastic surgery. No, I've never heard of Tenneson, and I don't really care to hear about him. I expect you to concentrate fully on this rotation! That is all, Mr. Maizel! Once again, please vacate yourself from my office! Now!"

As the medical student trudged out of the office, he muttered something incomprehensible under his breath and made his way toward the internal medicine floor.

8

After replacing the phone on its cradle, a pretty, short-haired, middle-aged nurse said, "Jack, you got another one coming up from the admissions office in about ten minutes."

Jack Maizel gave a deep sigh. "Look, first of all, you need to call me doctor, okay? Not Jack. It's unprofessional, and besides I earned that title. And second, I've already done three medical histories and physicals for the night, so I'm going to take a break. The new one's just gonna have to wait!"

The nurse sighed in disgust. "You're not a doctor yet, Jack! You're just a medical student, remember? So please, Jack, humor me! She's traveled all the way from Corbin. You know, that's about a two-hour drive. I'm sure she's tired and hungry. And you know we can't do anything to comfort her until you finish your clinical workup and assessment and give us some preliminary orders. Please, just—"

"Look, *nurse*! I'm the *doctor*, damn it!" Jack said, raising his voice. "I tell you what to do. You don't tell me! I told you I'm taking a break! I don't give a crap if she's tired or not. Those eastern Kentucky hillbillies don't know the first thing of being tired because they don't fricking do any work. I'm exhausted, and I'm just not doing her until I get some-thing to eat, watch a little TV, and rest awhile. For God's sake, I've got all night!"

The nurse looked at him for a moment, shrugged, and walked away, making remarks about being in a bad mood, medical students being arrogant, horrible, and just nasty kids.

"And I told you to call me *doctor*!"

Jack knew he shouldn't act out this way. It only made him look bad, and other people would use it as ammunition against him. That was what the psychologist told him. Through the years of counseling and anger management exercises after the Ajax incident, it finally started to help until his parents talked him into going to medical school. This was something he just did not want to do, so he began to act out more. Whenever he slipped into those foul moods, it was usually centered on his parents, annoying and needy patients, or when he was excessively tired—in that order.

9

"Okay, wake up!" Jack Maizel said as he walked into the patient's room some two hours after she had been admitted. He felt crappy and tired, especially after the tongue-lashing he had gotten from his attending and getting slammed with patients all night. The student was in no mood to socialize—just get the work done and get to bed.

He plopped himself down on the bedside chair and scooted it away from the patient, making a loud screeching noise against the tile floor.

"I'm Dr. Maizel, and I'm going to work you up. Your name's Dixon, right?"

The patient looked up at him with a gentle but apprehensive smile. "You don't look like a doctor to me. In fact, you look like you're barely out of high school. You remind me of a little boy I once saw holding on to his momma's hand tight on the first day of grade school. You could tell that he was so scared, bless his little heart. Yes, you look just like that little boy!"

Perturbed and feeling as if the patient was condescending to him, Jack instantly changed his demeanor. "Look, lady, I don't need that crap tonight! From you or anyone else! So, cool it, okay? I'm here to see why you're here and what we need to do. Just cooperate and answer my questions." Jack fiercely stared at the patient for a few silent seconds. "Now, how old are you?"

"My heavens, did the squirrels eat your nuts or what? Why are you pitching such a hissy fit? You know down where I live, we'd say that you're lower than a snake's belly in a wagon rut! I still don't believe you're a doctor. You look like somebody's little boy. That's it! I think I'll call you Sonny Boy. Yup, you look just like a sonny boy to me! Momma's sonny boy!"

Jack Maizel was tired, and he gave the woman a look of disgust. He was now burning with rage. "That's it. I don't need to take this from you or anyone else. You don't answer my questions—you don't get any food tonight, and you don't get your welcome package!"

Jack rose from his chair, screeching it again, and shut the patient's chart loudly. "I'll come back later when you're less feisty and more cooperative. Maybe you'll listen and answer some of my questions a little bit better when you're hungry!"

With that, he stormed out and slammed the door.

Mildred Dixon stared at the door and had a sunken feeling in her heart. She didn't mean to make him feel badly, but she was nervous and just wanted someone to feel compassion for her. She had been anxious and scared of the unknown. Coming to the big city she wasn't used to and going on this journey to see what was wrong with her belly—it had been such a long day. Mildred began to cry. At first a few sobs, but then she couldn't stop and continued to cry until her nose became full. She got to the point where she couldn't breathe, and her eyes became so swollen and red that it was difficult to see.

Mildred just wanted to go home. She didn't want anything to do with the big medical center or anyone in it. It was too big and so impersonal. Besides, just because it was big didn't mean that they knew everything. Certainly, they aren't very nice folks here. Why couldn't she just have her tests done at home? That way, she wouldn't have to meet up with such nasty people like Sonny Boy.

He didn't seem to be a bad person. He was more like a lost soul. *I wonder if he treated all his patients that way?* thought Mildred. *If so, how can he act the way he does? How can anyone tolerate him as a doctor? He has so much to learn about life and social skills. Yes, that's it, social skills! Maybe I can teach him a thing or two about how to be nicer to people before I leave here.*

She prayed silently, desperately wanting to be with Delbert. *Why aren't you with me, now? I need you so, my dear love.*

10

Loud music, people talking, shouting, and laughing. Glasses and dishes clanging. The noise was so loud that individual sounds could not be clearly untangled. It combined to create its own disharmony.

Women wore such heavy makeup that it looked as if it was painted on. Most of the men were military—many from Fort Knox and some from Bowman Field, the nearby civilian airport that became a training center for the US Army Air Forces.

People were dancing, eating, and drinking, and a few couples even found corner spots to kiss and make out, while some went a little further to pursue a more intimate activity.

Smoke from cigars and cigarettes filled rooms, accented by strong perfume fragrances, the smell of liquor, and body odors—many partiers passed out.

Mildred Dixon was miserable. She wasn't sure why people saw this as fun. It was hot, it stank, she couldn't breathe or think clearly, and now with a roaring appetite, she just wanted to have a nice dinner. That was what she thought she was going to—a dinner party.

She never expected such a boisterous party. Helen made it sound like it was only a few couples for dinner and perhaps even a chance to meet some eligible men up from the army base or from Bowman Field, where airmen were being trained as B-17 bomber crews.

She didn't cross paths with Helen, not even once, since they had entered the hotel after rudely dismissing the boys in the taxi. Mildred felt badly about that and wanted to get to know the man with the dark hair. But Helen insisted they get into the dinner party quickly.

As she was thinking about the evening and how gloomy she was, a tap on the shoulder startled her. A man loudly asked, "What's your name?"

Mildred turned around and exclaimed, "Heavens to Betsy!"

The man, cupping his right ear, smiled. "Your name is Betsy?"

It was him! The beautiful man from the cab! Mildred could not believe her luck. He was naturally soft-spoken and hard to hear, but Mildred paid very close attention to what the man said. "Well, my name is Bert. Officially it's Delbert Vines. So, nice to meet you, Betsy!"

Bewildered, astonished, and elated at the same time, she couldn't stop smiling. As hard as she tried, she couldn't get any words out. She knew her face was flushed and not from the alcohol, either. "No, I'm not Betsy, I'm Mildred Dixon. Betsy is just a figure of speech, silly." She chuckled. "I was startled by the tap and surprised to see you once again—so soon!"

"What?" Bert cupped both ears. "I cannot hear you well. It is too loud. I can pick up only about every other word you're saying. Let's get out of here, if you don't mind, so we can hear each other and maybe get some clean air into our lungs."

She nodded enthusiastically. He grabbed her hands and led her out. His grip was firm. She could feel the hard callouses on his palms, but the back of his hand was soft and comforting.

Once they were outside, Bert said, "Hey, I heard the Ohio River is straight down Fourth Street. Let's take a stroll to the riverbanks and have ourselves a nice chat."

At that moment, she was happy. Her hunger pangs disappeared, and she couldn't think of anything else but this man. She knew Cupid had shot his arrows—and it must have been hundreds of them shot all at once.

Just then, she stopped. Her smile was replaced by a frown. "Mr. Delbert, I want to apologize for my friend's bad behavior with the cab incident—"

The man waved his hand. "No, it was a gas! I cracked up. It all happened so quickly it took my buddy, Van—Van Miller—a minute to figure out what happened and how we got had. He's a practical joker himself but got played good by your friend, and he wasn't happy about it. I laughed so hard it instantly put me in a good mood."

"Well, I'm glad you aren't mad with us. So, all this time, you were coming to the same party as we were? Why didn't you say so in the cab?"

"I guess we were. We just didn't know where the party was. A fella in our squadron mentioned there was a big party on Broadway at the Brown and that if we wanted to meet some gals, we should go. Miller jumped at it without getting more details and somehow dragged me along. He didn't know where we were going, either. We didn't know the Brown was a hotel! We thought it was a street. You know Broadway and Brown or something like that!"

"Oh, that's so funny. So, what's the dope on you two? You are airmen, I suppose? At Bowman Field?"

"Yes. We are training as teams to fly on the B-17 bombers. I'm a bombardier and Miller is trained as a navigator. He comes across as a knucklehead, but he's a real ace when he gets in that big ol' bomber! He gets us anywhere and always on time!"

"What does a bombardier do, Mr. Delbert?"

"Hey, the name is Bert. Delbert is just an official name to put on birth certificates, high school diplomas, college degrees, and probably on my gravestone one day!"

Mildred looked sad for a second. "Bert, I cannot ever see you being in a grave. I know with the world the way it is—those conflicts and all—we can never know from one day to the next, but you are too smooth of a man to not live your life out fully. So perfect, you are! I think you have angels fluttering all around you, like hummingbirds floating around flowers."

"Well, thank you, Mildred." He paused for a moment. "Mildred, I have never said this to anyone because I have never met anyone like you.

The instant I saw you in the cab, I was smitten. You know, lovestruck! I don't know why, and I don't know how. I don't really care about the logistics—I just know that I am in love with you."

He kissed her on the cheek. She smelled so good.

Mildred looked away for a second to compose herself, caught a tear rolling from her right eye, then smiled. Without uttering a sound, she reached for his lips with hers and they embraced. After a long kiss, she gently pushed him back. "So what does a bombardier do?"

11

After about an hour of crying and intermittent dozing off, there was a soft knock on the door. A man wearing a short, white clinician's jacket with a stethoscope looped over the back of his neck ambled into the patient's room.

"Hello. You are Miss Mildred Dixon, correct?"

The dark-skinned man, lanky with a posture as straight and erect as any California redwood, looked imposing at first glance, but his gentle and melodic voice would instantly lull a crying baby to sleep and soften an anxious adult.

"My name is Ahgri Zuri, and I am a fourth-year medical student doing an acting internship rotation for the month of September."

He smiled warmly as he offered her a handshake.

"I am aware that another student, my acting intern colleague, visited you earlier, but I do not believe he was able to finish the admission medical history or the physical examination. As perhaps you are aware, if you do not have a note and orders posted in your patient chart, the nurses will not be able to perform their duties and thus will certainly be unable to take proper care of you.

"The nurses were concerned and wanted you to be comfortable, so they contacted me to see if I could—how do you say it—get the ball rolling. Thus, I would like to conduct a brief interview and a quick physical exam to get some things started." He paused. "With your permission, of course, Miss Mildred?" Another pause. "On second thought, I apologize, I should have asked if I may call you Miss Mildred? It is such a pretty name."

Mildred's cheeks warmed as she nodded, confused by the sudden turn of events.

"My colleague, whom you have already met, will complete a more comprehensive history and examination tomorrow. So, if you do not terribly mind and if my intrusion upon your solitude and privacy is not too inconvenient for you, may we please commence with the process?"

Mildred could not help but smile and stare at the young man. "You are so kind to explain this to me in such a nice way. Your voice is so gentle, and you speak so properly. Where do you come from, sir?" The patient suddenly put her hands to her mouth. "Oh my, I am so sorry. My poor manners. I don't mean to be rude. I just want to know what nationality you hail from?"

Ahgri chuckled and broke out into a wide grin. He placed his hands over hers and patted them. "It's quite all right, my dear lady. I was born in Tanzania—a country in East Africa. I was fortunate enough to have been adopted by a British couple when I was younger. They spent much of their time in the United States because of their missionary work. However, much of my early education and upbringing was in Great Britain. So perhaps you detect a bit of my British accent and a small bit of a Tanzanian accent as well. Makes for an interesting, almost musical, delivery of my words, would you not say?"

"Well, you seem to be such a nice young man, unlike that other young brute of a boy impersonating a doctor. We didn't get off to a good start. He was rude, and I was tired and on a short fuse. I called him Sonny Boy, and I think it made him mad! He was so arrogant and acted like such a tyrant even though he looked like a dirty little boy who hadn't taken a bath in days. Very mischievous—you can just see it in his face! He made me very upset, but I feel sorry for him because I think he has some serious mental problems."

With a knowing look and a smile, Ahgri asked, "You are referring to my colleague, Jack Maizel, are you not? You have named him Sonny Boy?" His grin widened. "If so, that is humorous and fits him marvelously! Marvelously well! Touché, Miss Mildred! Well done!"

"Yes, that's the young . . . you know . . . punk, who came in earlier. He claimed that he's a doctor, but I knew better. I was a nurse for over thirty years at a small psychiatric hospital! He's just some boy faking being a doctor. Who knows, he's probably faked through everything he does in life. I have to tell you, I don't like him much, but I do feel sorry for him. I don't think he's a happy boy."

Ahgri smiled and said, "Yes, of course, I understand. He is, I think you Americans use the phrase, rough around the edges, especially when he gets busy. But, I can assure you, Miss Mildred, that Jack is a good man who has a good heart, but no one can see it because he covers it up with darkness and going overboard with his rudeness!"

"Well, he was nasty to me, but like I said, I think there is something wrong with him upstairs, if you know what I mean. The boy needs a lot of help."

After Ahgri did a brief interview and exam, he documented in Mildred Dixon's patient chart and wrote the admission note.

"*Lala vizuri*, Miss Dixon! That is 'sleep well' in my native language."

"Yes. That is Swahili, correct?" asked Mildred.

"Correct," replied Ahgri as he left.

Mildred got her midnight snack and some Tylenol for her pounding headache.

12

"We are patiently waiting for you, Mr. Maizel. So, if you would kindly grace us with your presentation of this patient, we would appreciate it," said Dr. William Jones, chairman of the Internal Medicine Department, in a sarcastic and patronizing tone.

Several students, medical residents, and nurses were converged in a huddle outside of patient room 628, awaiting the presentation of the newly admitted patient from last night.

As Jack looked through a handful of scribbled notes with no apparent order to them, Dr. Jones continued pompously: "As we are all aware, patient medical rounds are opportunities to convey your historical and physical findings to this group so that we may learn and teach each other the intricacies of medical care. This is the forum where we discuss planning for our patients. If it is not too terribly burdensome to you, *Mr.* Maizel, we would certainly like to hear about this new patient who bears the name Mildred Dixon from Corbin, Kentucky." Dr. Jones cleared his throat loudly. "Today, Mr. Maizel! Now!"

Jack Maizel was exhausted—too fatigued to think in a logical manner and too terribly worn out to go through an early morning participation of patient rounds. He just wanted to sleep. He knew Dr. Jones's reputation of being a relentless stickler for details and how he took on medical problems with vigor. The physician took extreme delight in drilling and embarrassing his students by asking difficult questions, then forcing them into discussing minute details by creating endless what-if scenarios about a medical case. He especially liked the interrogation style of questioning that reminded students of tortured prisoners in a war movie and even took delight when they could not answer or appeared nervous.

If a student lapsed on a particular topic, he would relentlessly chastise them in front of other students with the specific intent of humiliating them. He believed that this method would make them study harder to avoid being embarrassed during future interrogations. Most students did not pass through his rotation unscathed and neither would Jack Maizel.

The trouble with Jack was that he hadn't slept in two nights. He didn't have time to update patient charts or review the lab results of new patients, and so he was unprepared for the morning rounds—and Dr. Jones.

He fidgeted nervously, glancing at Ahgri with a look that said, "Help me out, man!" He looked through notebooks and note cards bound by rubber bands—even scraps of folded and crumpled paper that he retrieved from his clinical jacket pockets.

"Let's see," he said, looking for notes about this patient. At one point, a reflex hammer tumbled out of his chest pocket and bounced several times on the tiled floor before landing on Dr. Jones's right shoe.

Reactionary giggling and snickering temporarily broke the tension.

"Mr. Maizel! I said now!" Dr. Jones snapped. "What are you doing?"

Ignoring the question, Jack discovered a set of note cards in his right pants pocket and flipped through them until he came upon one marked "628." At the top, he had written the name Mildred Dixon and her age, sixty-three. Immediately underneath was written "spot on X-ray film—unknown etiology and needs workup." A wave of panic suddenly consumed him when he read and realized that he had forgotten to come back to finish the workup from the previous evening. He did not have a complete history, nor was a physical exam even started, not to mention any preliminary and routine lab work required for all new admissions. He simply had run out of time this morning.

"*Mr.* Maizel!"

Jack Maizel faked a cough, which was comically false. "The patient is a sixty-three-year-old white female from Corbin, Kentucky, who was referred directly to Dr. Jones by her local medical doctor. She was admitted last night as a direct admit to Six North, on the internal medicine floor, to be evaluated for unexplained weight loss and a suspicious lesion located in her midabdominal region."

He suddenly stopped. Silence ensued. Everyone in the group continued to look at him expectantly. But he did not say anything. He looked back at the group and Dr. Jones. A couple of the female nurses standing toward the back of the rounding team could not contain their quiet giggling as they attempted to muffle the sounds with their hands. A few snickers were also heard. Ahgri Zuri looked away, embarrassed for his friend but also feeling contempt for Jack's cavalier attitude for just about everything.

"Continue, Mr. Maizel!" said Dr. Jones. "What are you waiting for? I want to know if Ms. Dixon went through the emergency room before coming to my service and if she got any labs drawn or got any radiographical studies. Also, we want to hear about the patient's history of present illness, the review of systems, social history, family history, past medical history, and her physical exam—in case you have forgotten how to present a case. Then I want to hear about the laboratory data and finally your differential diagnosis and the plans for this patient. Proceed. Now! We are all patiently awaiting your discourse, *Mr.* Maizel."

"Um. Ah. Uh, yeah . . . I really don't know what to say, Dr. Jones. She was a direct admit to the floor and bypassed our ER. We got some admission labs but don't have any results yet." Jack avoided everyone's stares by looking at the floor, shoulders slightly slumped forward. After a moment of silence, he said, "I, uh, guess I forgot this patient and just didn't have time to finish Dixon."

A thunder of laughter erupted. Only Dr. Jones and Ahgri did not participate. Dr. Jones pulled out the patient's chart from the rolling chart rack and leafed through the documents.

"I see there is an admission note and a set of update notes . . . but curiously they are not written by you, Mr. Maizel! Mr. Zuri, why did you write these notes when clearly Mr. Maizel was responsible for this patient's care?"

"I saw that he was overwhelmed with patients last night, Dr. Jones, and I was just trying to assist him. Besides, I was concerned the patient did not have diet and symptomatic medications ordered, as well as specific medications she may already be on. I wanted to make sure that they were ordered in case she had a difficult evening."

Without losing his composure, Dr. Jones looked sternly at Jack. "Are there any other patients that you have forgotten or didn't finish, Mr. Maizel?"

"Ah, let me think . . ." Jack looked through his note cards. "I don't think so. I mean, uh, no sir. Well, there might have been a couple more. But I think I've done everyone else." He looked uncertain. "I'm not a hundred percent sure."

More laughter.

"Okay! Then we shall proceed to the other patients, and after we have completed our rounds, you will spend the rest of your morning hours in my office explaining why and how you forgot and didn't finish your responsibilities to our patients. After that, you will go to Ms. Dixon and apologize to her for your, what I believe is, early onset dementia or, more than likely, an innate lack of responsibility marred by arrogance and conceit! Then you will spend the rest of the afternoon working her up, including drawing all the blood work and performing the scut work yourself. Then you, Mr. Maizel, and I will round on Ms. Dixon. You will tell me everything about her medical history. Nothing will be left out. Do you understand me, Mr. Maizel?"

"Yeah, sure. No, I mean . . . yes, sir! Sure!" Jack's voice crackled slightly, trying to sound enthusiastic but failing miserably.

Dr. Jones didn't say anything but shot daggers into Jack's eyes, causing him to look away in embarrassment. Finally, Dr. Jones looked at his patients' rounding team and ordered, "I am ending this rounding session for now. I want my medicine residents to meet me at my office in an hour. I will have you update me on each of our patients, and we will go over the day's management plans."

He then turned to Jack. "Mr. Maizel, follow me down this hall-way!"

Jack had a difficult time following the rapid marching cadence of Dr. Jones as they walked past the nurses' station to a semi-remote area at the end of the ward unit.

"Mr. Maizel, I do not like you, and I do not like your attitude, your sloppiness, your disrespectful demeanor, and your lack of com-passion for anyone and seemingly everything!" Dr. Jones gave him a hard stare, then said, "Look, you are a smart man. I know you are in the top third of your class as far as test scores go and I know that you are very adept with various medical procedures, but in my opinion, you should not be in medical school, and I consider it a sin that our medical admissions committee admitted you to our fine medical school to become a doctor. In my opinion, that was a faulty decision on their part! You may be smart, and you may be technically savvy, but your attitude stinks, Mr. Maizel!

"The only reason I am not harder on you and why I have given you any leeway at all is because of your dad. He was a good friend of mine in medical school, and he is one of the finest cardiovascular surgeons around. We owe each other favors, but let me tell you, mister, I will not sacrifice patient safety and risk patient neglect and disrespect by one of my students just to satisfy a few favors. I think your dad would agree with me on that. So, as they say, either shape up—real fast now—or I will ship you out with my boot print on your rear end! So, get your ass in gear, mister. See me in my office in exactly ten minutes; then you will spend the next few hours getting to know your patient! That will be all!"

13

After Dr. Jones abruptly ended rounds and dismissed the team, everyone scattered and went their separate ways. Jack needed to talk to Ahgri and went straight to him after the tongue-lashing by Dr. Jones.

Ahgri was as impeccably dressed and spotless as ever in his white clinical jacket, a stethoscope neatly draped and dangling over his neck. Jack owned only one clinical jacket, and it had a mixed bag of stains on it from infrequent washing. They were engaged in a deep conversation when one of the ward clerks called out.

"Well, if it ain't Mutt and Jeff! Hanging out at our nurses' station! We love Jeff but not so much Mutt! No, I'm sorry! Let me take it back. We don't like Mutt at all! Not one smidgen!"

Those standing around the nurses' station howled with laughter, but it did not deter Ahgri and Jack. Ahgri, who usually seemed calm, now had a perturbed tone to his voice and was irritated. "What is wrong with you, Jack? Why do you constantly get in trouble and stay in trouble? It is as if you just do not care about anything or any person. How do you live that way?"

"Come on, Ahgri! I was up all night with a bunch of admissions. I feel like a mangy cat with a bunch of fleas. Yeah, I'm the cat, and the patients and people like Jones are the fleas. They are annoying, and they're pests! I just want to say, 'Get out of my life, you damn buggers! Leave me the hell alone!'"

He took a deep breath, closed his eyes tight, and shook his head. "Look, I don't like this field of work they call medicine, all right? I told you that before. And you know I don't want to be a doctor, and I can't stand dealing with sick and needy people. My dad told me to just go into cosmetic surgery because I'll make good money. But I don't care about the money. I pretend that I do to appease my parents. My folks are rich as hell, so I can go on my own and do what I really want to do if I can get the money from them. I'm not sure if this is worth it, Ahgri."

At first, Ahgri looked at Jack as if he had lost his soul and needed help from some televangelist. Then he said, "*Kila ndege huruka na mbawa zake.*" He shook his head. "Jack, do you not understand anything about life? I've explained this proverb to you before. It means, 'every bird flies with its own wings.'" Without waiting for an answer, he kept talking. "Do you understand what that means, Jack? It means that you have to be your own person. You are unhappy because your parents dictate your life. Yes, you have said to me many times you do not want to be a doctor. If you use someone else's wings, such as your parents, then you will never fly, my friend. In other words, you will never succeed!

"I have described parts of my life to you over the past few years, and you know I worked on coffee plantations when I was a child. That was right before my mountain climbing days where I assisted many others as a guide up Kili. To work at coffee plantations is such hard work, but I learned so much about life. A very important lesson I once learned was about insects and coffee trees.

"First, you know that I detest sloppiness and untidiness. Most likely it is a result of my genetic makeup. Thus, slovenly behavior and disorganization have always bothered me! That is why I am always annoyed with you, Jack! You are the sloppiest, most untidy, and most disorganized man I have ever met! I think you, most likely, sleep in your clothes, which are never washed, and you hardly ever take a bath! It is disgusting. If you think I am the only one who believes that about you, then just ask any of these nurses here!"

Ahgri shut his eyes for a second and shook his head slightly. Then he sighed deeply. "I want to tell you a story about the coffee bean trees. The arabica coffee trees in Tanzania always had a lot of weeds underneath them. They were quite unsightly and on my first day on the job, as a young boy, I started clearing the underbrush of each tree. The overseer saw this and began yelling at me: 'No, no, no, don't ever clear the weeds from the trees! What is wrong with you?' I was scared because I grew up in an environment where no one ever yelled at me for cleaning, picking up clutter, and straightening up messes.

"He said, 'You are destroying all the beneficial insects! They eat the insects that eat at the coffee bean trees, and they live in the weeds underneath the plants. If you clean up the weeds, you destroy the good insects.'"

Jack looked dismayed. "So, what's that got to do with anything, man? That's the dumbest story ever!"

His friend responded patiently. "I'm not done yet. You, in this story, are the coffee bean tree, my friend. The beneficial insects are the patients and our purported nemesis, Dr. Jones. They are nasty looking, creepy, and they seem to annoy you. They are deemed pests in your life, correct? But, nevertheless, they are good for you, Jack! They are there to help *you* and make *you* into a good, strong, and healthy coffee bean tree. You learn to accept them and to learn from them. Even to love them. They will not eat away at your soul, but they will nourish you. They are good for you, so learn to embrace them! Not all pests are bad.

"I am very sorry to tell you this part, Jack, but I fear that those people who your parents know and seem to be your friends and say they want to help you do so because your parents are rich and influential. They are bad insects! Behind your back, you can be sure they care nothing about you and would do nothing to help if you were ever to become poor and destitute. They are evil insects, and they will destroy you—the coffee bean tree would never flourish because those evil insects would eat it up!

"Yes, Dr. Jones detests people like Dr. Tenneson, your purported friend, but Jones knows that people like him are all about themselves. They care nothing for you. Tenneson pays attention to you because your family's name will draw in more patients to him. So, he is just using you! A bad insect, indeed, my friend. A very bad bug! You must please remember that. Much of life is about this concept, Jack!"

"I guess I'm confused, Ahgri. First you tell me that I'm a sloppy guy and that I'm disgusting. So, I think you're likening me to the bad bugs, but then you're saying good things about the people I don't like and bad things about the people who are supposed to like me. I just don't get it, man!"

Ahgri took in another deep breath. "Okay, Jack, what I'm saying is metaphorical and slightly abstract but not that difficult to understand. The bottom line, as accountants would say, is that not all insects are alike. There are good ones and bad ones. Embrace the good insects like Dr. Jones, Miss Mildred, and even some of the nurses. They will be beneficial to you. Avoid the bad ones because they will destroy you. As for you, my friend"—Ahgri smiled now—"if you are an insect, you are a good insect on the inside but a bad one on the outside. Take a bath, shave, and wash your hair. Lose some weight as well, my friend. You will feel better, and you will appear like a good insect on the outside. And finally remember, Jack, every bird flies with its own wings. Not another bird's wings but its own.

"Now, you better make your way to Dr. Jones's office or you will be doubly punished, I fear!"

14

After the verbal beating from the chairman of internal medicine and the philosophical talk from his best friend, Jack thought he had better at least try to change his attitude and approach to life. But it was hard. Circumstances in life kept him obstinate and cantankerous, and he simply had a difficult time being nice. The killing of his horse, Ajax, when he was twelve and the insistence of his rich parents that he go to medical school left him confused and with a habit to lash out at anyone—even those who tried to help, like Ahgri. Sometimes, no matter how hard he tried to self-regulate his behavior, his temper would just flare up and he would become cynical, mean, and rude.

Just before Jack entered room 628, he smoothed his clinical jacket and straightened the collar. The jacket was downright claustrophobic, and the paraphernalia and notebooks that cluttered the oversize pockets were heavy and clumsy. It reminded him of circus monkeys that danced around in silly outfits, complete with the small, round fezzes held on to their heads with straps under their chins.

The attending physicians all wore long white coats, which were a bit intimidating to students and patients alike, but they made them look important and, somehow, smarter.

His preferred self-image, however, was to don surgical scrubs. They were like pajamas—loose and comfortable—more like him. Besides, no matter what you did with them—wad them up or sleep in them—they never got wrinkled.

As Jack walked in, he kept telling himself, *I'm not going to let this lady get on my bad side.*

"Well, Dixon, are you ready to talk now?" Jack's tone was neutral. It was easy to detect that this was forced, but he got through it.

Mildred was facing away from the door, sitting on the edge of her bed and staring out the window overlooking a parking lot. She continued to sit motionless without acknowledging him.

He sighed deeply, working hard to keep his temper in check. "Look, Dixon, do I have to walk out on you again, or are you going to please cooperate this time? I don't have time for these juvenile games!"

"Oh, it's you, Sonny Boy. I didn't hear you call out my name. I thought you said Dixon instead of *Miss* Dixon, so I wasn't sure if you were talking to me or just talking about a person named Dixon to someone. You do know that Dixon rhymes with Nixon, and when Richard Nixon was president, most people referred to him as Nixon when they talked *about* him, but when *they asked him questions*, they usually yelled out *Mr.* President or *President* Nixon. They showed some sense of respect. When you yell out Dixon as if it is some inanimate object, that is disrespectful. So, did you mean to call me *Ms.* or *Miss* Dixon?"

She did not look at the young medical student but continued to gaze out the window as if searching for something. "And something else, I do know that you won't leave this time because your boss will get on you again. And you, Sonny Boy, cannot afford to have him mad at you any longer. I may be old, but I hear well, and I heard you getting in trouble this morning," she said with a chuckle. "It was actually wonderful to hear that you got what was coming to you!"

Jack Maizel felt his face burn hot, embarrassed by what she knew. However, it left almost as quickly as it appeared. He walked by the bedside and, instead of sitting, plopped his left knee on a chair and rested the same-side elbow on it while placing his other hand on his waist. "Okay, Dixon, can we just do this civilly so I can get some rest before tonight?"

"Why certainly, Sonny Boy!"

Mildred could tell that "Sonny Boy" perturbed and agitated him. So as long as he acted this way toward her and called her by only her last name, she would call him Sonny Boy. She finally turned around and smiled as she laid down on the bed and propped herself up slightly with two pillows.

Taking a deep breath and trying to hold his temper down, he said, "Okay, let's start from the beginning, Dixon. Why are you here?"

Mildred looked at him, not a malicious gaze but a look of some amazement, and replied pleasantly, "Pray tell, young man, what became of your manners? Why is it so hard to give respect to someone? You will call me Miss Dixon from now on!"

Jack looked the other way, shrugged, and said, "Sure, why not? Okay, so we got that out of the way. What brings you here, *Miss* Dixon?"

"Well, my doctor at home sent me here for some test."

"What made him want to get tests on you?"

"I'm not exactly sure, but I had some pain in my belly and had lost some weight, so I decided to go see Dr. Weaver. He's my family doctor, you know—down in Corbin. Anyway, he did a lot of blood work and even took some X-rays of my belly. He told me that I needed more tests and that I should see a specialist. So that's why I'm here."

"When d'ya start turning yellow?" he asked indifferently without looking at her.

"What do you mean?"

"Well, you're a little jaundice looking. So, when did you become jaundice?"

"I didn't know that I looked that way," she replied with surprise and concern.

"Come on, Dixon, don't you look at yourself in the mirror? Yeah, okay, you're not as yellow as a pumpkin yet, but I can tell. Didn't your doctor in the mountains tell you that? How 'bout your friends? Didn't they say anything?"

Mildred immediately got up and walked toward the bathroom and stared at herself in the mirror. She whispered, "Oh my."

Jack straightened up, sighed, looked at his watch, and said, "Look, Dixon, today's the second day of September. I got twenty-nine more days this month to put up with this rotation, so don't make it difficult for me. Can you come back so I can get done with you?"

"Thirty days hath September," the woman replied, continuing to look at herself in the mirror.

"What's that? Meaning what?"

She turned around to face him. "I said, thirty days hath September. Today's the second. You have twenty-eight more days, not twenty-nine, as you said." She turned back around to once again look at her reflection in the mirror.

"What the h—I mean what are you talking about, lady?"

"Sonny Boy, every school child knows the poem to remember the number of days in the months. It goes like this:

> Thirty days hath September,
> April, June, and November.
> All the rest have thirty-one,
> Excepting February alone,
> And that has twenty-eight days clear
> And twenty-nine in each leap year."

She smirked and said, "Now where were you when they taught that in grade school?"

Jack Maizel did not respond to her question, but with an increasing annoyance in his voice, truly disliking this woman, he simply said, "I need to finish my interview and check you over, so can you come back to bed? My attending's waiting for me."

15

OFFICE OF THE INTERNAL MEDICINE CHAIRMAN,
WILLIAM D. JONES, MD, PHD

A. B. CHANDLER MEDICAL CENTER

LEXINGTON, KENTUCKY

After spending more than two hours with the patient, completing the history and physical exam, Jack Maizel called the hospital operator to page Dr. Jones. *I think my spending two hours with the patient and getting a good history will satisfy Jones,* he reasoned. *That short talk with Jones was brutal and I don't want to do that again!*

* * *

"You may proceed, Mr. Maizel. And please do be concise," ordered Dr. Jones. "I have all day, but you, unfortunately, do not." He looked at his watch. "You will have to be back on call in approximately one hour, and I'm sure this presentation and our subsequent discussion will take that long. I believe that there are three new patients already waiting for you to complete an admissions workup for later tonight. After this week, you should be quite experienced at admitting new internal medicine patients and presenting them to a group. Remember this always, Mr. Maizel: From difficulties comes perfection. You may now proceed!"

Jack fantasized about punching the man in the nose. Then, when he had him down for the count, he would pounce on him like a crazed and rabid animal, choking the old guy. He hated—no, he despised—the man. How conceited can a person be? But, for now, he had to play the good student game so that he could get out of this rotation alive and pursue his dreams—er, his parents' dreams for him—of living a life as a surgeon. His parents would be proud that he became a Kentucky blue-blood doctor. Yes, he would have a good life, even better than his parents. Very soon! Well, that was what his parents wanted, anyway.

But sadly, he still struggled with the notion of being the doctor his parents wished for him. It was his cardiovascular surgeon father's idea, and his mother went along with it since it gave her even greater prestige and clout among her circle of rich and influential friends. She delighted in talking about how her medical school son will become the best plastic surgeon in town. How he'd be able to turn a prune back into a plum.

Jack knew that he was not destined to be that glorious doctor his mother wanted him to be. He realized after much introspection that his attitude was bad, and it was mainly because of the forced occupational goal set by his parents. It seemed no matter how hard Jack struggled to control his behavior, he just couldn't get past the rebellious, anti-just-about-everything personality he harbored. "I just don't want to be a doctor!" he kept telling his parents. "I don't like needy, sick, and whiny people. Most of them do it to themselves by getting fat and not caring about anything except how they can have entertainment, eat a lot of junk food, and drink a lot of liquor! I just want to be around my horses in the peace and quiet of open pastureland! They are innocent and beautiful creatures, but people just use them for their own pleasure."

He argued constantly about what he viewed as hypocrisy of the horse race industry. "You use these beautiful animals to make money for yourselves. Sure, they are well groomed and every detail of their health and well-being are meticulously taken care of and even some love is given, but as soon as they get hurt while making money for you, then—*poof*—you just get rid of them! That's just not right! I want to do something more to protect these sweet creatures! I want to advocate for their welfare!"

His parents did not want to buy into his dreams of being an animal rights activist and running an animal sanctuary that specialized in horses. They were appalled when he first announced his intentions as a high school freshman. "You can't make money and live a good life doing that!" his mother had said. "You're a smart guy! You need to be a doctor! A plastic surgeon. The best in Lexington!"

He knew that if he disobeyed their wishes, it would be antithetical to his parents' social structure that helped fuel their need for prosperity, not to mention showcase their wealth. He wondered if they might cut off financial support and put him out to pasture if he didn't go along with their plans for him.

Despite these conflicts, Jack felt bad that he always seemed to be rude, but he was in a bad place because of his parents' desires and not his. When medical school started, he decided that he was going to be antisocial and avoid the do-gooders and ass-kissers of his classmates. He couldn't help it.

In psychology class, he learned how medical folks labeled people like him. *Acting out* was the more descriptive layman's term, but the psychologists liked to call it oppositional defiant disorder, or ODD.

ODD! Yeah, he thought, *that fits me perfectly.* He was "odd" compared to his classmates and all the professors, nurses, and everyone knew it. He just didn't fit in. Ahgri was the only person who ever listened to him and understood what Jack was going through.

"Mr. Maizel! Are you going to speak or are you going to just sit there and daydream?"

"Okay, Dr. Jones. Sorry." Jack cleared his throat, slightly nervous. "The lady's a sixty-three-year-old—"

"Does the *lady* have a name, Mr. Maizel?" Dr. Jones interjected, looking agitated and tense.

"Mildred Dixon is a sixty-three-year-old white female referred by the PMD with a—"

"I don't understand what a PMD is, Mr. Maizel. There will be no abbreviations in the presentations with me. Understood?"

"Yeah." Jack was more perturbed than ever, but quickly changed his reply. "Yes, sir. Mildred Dixon is a sixty-three-year-old white female referred by her private medical doctor for further evaluation of unexplained weight loss, abdominal pain, and mild hepatomegaly. The patient was in her usual good state of health until several months ago. At that time, she started to have some vague abdominal pains primarily in the epigastric and the right upper quadrant areas—"

"Mr. Maizel!"

"Yes, sir?"

"When you say several months, what exactly do you mean? Do you mean three months or seven months? More or less?"

"Dixon couldn't remember."

"Mr. Maizel! What sort of respect is that? To call a patient, especially someone your elder, by their last name? She is not cattle waiting in line to be slaughtered! She is a human being. Treat her with dignity! Even I call you *Mister*. Don't ever let me hear you speak of a patient in that manner again! Do you understand me, Mr. Maizel?"

"Yes, sir." Jack now felt as if he'd been punched, beaten up, chewed on, and spat out, not the other way around as he had daydreamed.

"So, you don't know exactly how long the symptoms have been going on, is that correct?"

"Oh, yeah, I just remembered. It was two months. She started losing weight about the same time she was having abdominal pains. Can I continue?"

Dr. Jones simply nodded. "But before you go on, Mr. Maizel, did you quantify the amount of weight loss by history? How much weight loss are we talking about?"

"The weight loss occurred without any dietary aid and was unintentional. During this period, she also experienced occasional nausea, vomiting, and frequent back pain. I didn't ask about how much weight she lost. The back pain was described as starting in the abdominal area, which radiated to her back. With the continued pain, she sought the advice of her PMD—er—I mean private medical doctor. Whereupon he discovered a slight hepatomegaly on the physical exam.

"Initial gastrointestinal X-rays revealed some distortion of the duodenal loop, suggesting a possible lesion. Amylase and lipase at the doctor's office were slightly elevated, too. My physical exam revealed—"

"Excuse me, Mr. Maizel, but I did not hear anything about the past medical history, review of systems, or social and family history. I believe they come before the physical exam so that I may get a better picture of this patient. And also, I have a comment about not knowing how much weight she had lost before you go on. This is vital information to know in this case. Weight loss histories in the elderly is a significant problem and warrants an entire medical workup. Make sure you remember that, Mr. Maizel!"

"Sure, I understand. Yeah, sure, Dr. Jones. Can I proceed?"

There was a momentary silence. "Please do. But I want to interject for a moment. Do you know what the most important aspect of the physician-patient interaction is, Mr. Maizel?"

"Fund of knowledge," Jack replied.

"No, far from it, Mr. Maizel. It is the ability to listen. Not listen to just hear, but listen with intent and interest. Feel what they say and how they say it. You can get so much information from this. The practice of medicine is more an art than a science. The art portion will help you understand the deep pain, anxiety, or concerns your patients have. Don't be a robot or a machine. Listen with compassion. It is the hallmark of becoming a good doctor. Okay, you may proceed."

"Well, the past medical history is noncontributory. Ms. Dixon has never been sick in her life except the usual stuff like colds and belly aches. No surgeries, no hospitalizations. She's as healthy as a horse! The review of systems, other than what's in the history of present illness, is also noncontributory. I didn't really get into the social or family history with her too deeply. No one cares about that anyway!"

"And why not, Mr. Maizel?"

"Well, it has nothing to do with her illness. I think there's an outside chance she's got either colon cancer or stomach cancer, but more than likely, she's got something mild, like peptic ulcer disease, going on. I suppose she could have something more serious, but I doubt it with her initial presentation. I don't think it matters what her social or family history has to do with it."

Dr. Jones stared intensely at the young medical student and did not say anything for a long while. He then asked, "Did you know that smokers have about a two to two and a half times greater incidence of pancreatic cancer than their nonsmoking counterparts? Smoking is part of social history, Mr. Maizel. Does Ms. Dixon smoke? What does she do for a living?

Do you have no interest in this person as a human being? Is she just a science project for you, Mr. Maizel? A science project with no humanity? Social history is enormously important. It gives us a picture of her life and may give us clues to help us with our diagnosis. Is she married? Does she have children? What does she do for fun? What are her hobbies?"

"No, sir. I just didn't think it was that important."

"The social history, neglected by many medical students, residents, and physicians even with years of experience, is just as important a component of the complete history and physical exam as any other part of the document. In fact, I would say without detailed information about the social history, we could end up being caught up in a bind. For example, did Ms. Dixon recently travel anywhere? Did she go to a third-world country and perhaps picked up hepatitis A from food or water? What if Ms. Dixon had no family members living nearby who could check on her? And let's say she has to go on chemotherapy or becomes debilitated for a time. It would be nice to know her family or social support structure. Does she have transportation capabilities? What is her education level? Is she able to comprehend some of the esoteric medical aspects of her health management? When we send her home, will she need a home health aide? Is she able to consent to medical procedures? Do we know anything about her personal life? Does she have someone else with power of health-care attorney for decisions in case she suddenly lapses into an unconscious state? Is she destitute? Can she even afford some of the medicine or equipment we may need to send her home on? The list goes on and on, Mr. Maizel. So, yes, with absolute certainty, you will need to complete that portion of the history. Never neglect it again!"

Dr. Jones sighed and slightly nodded to Jack, signaling him to proceed.

"The physical exam revealed a somewhat mildly overweight individual who appeared slightly jaundiced. Remarkable findings were a palpable hepatic edge that was approximately two and a half centimeters below the right costal margin with mild tenderness upon palpation. Otherwise, the physical exam was totally within normal limits."

Jack looked at his professor, expecting to be asked more questions. But none came, so he proceeded.

"I have ordered a CBC with a differential, a repeat serum amylase and lipase. I also ordered a serum alkaline phosphatase with a complete metabolic panel. Fasting serum glucose and urinalysis for the morning. I ordered hemoccult testing of the stools, too."

"Okay, Mr. Maizel. I want to know what your differential diagnosis is, however, that part of your presentation should come prior to the plan portion." Dr. Jones stood erect, looking more like royalty than a professor of medicine.

"My working diagnosis, as I mentioned earlier, is either colon cancer or some type of stomach cancer. Could be peptic ulcer disease or could be something far-fetched. I don't think she has anything else, Dr. Jones."

"That's fine to think that, but you should always have multiple alternative diagnoses that should be running through your mind. Sometimes the symptoms may be red herrings, and it will lead you down the wrong path for your workup. I want you to do some reading tonight between your admissions and give me at least three other potential differential diagnoses in the morning." He looked at Jack for a moment. "I want to read your daily SOAP notes also. If you don't remember how to write a SOAP note, Mr. Maizel, *S* stands for subjective information, the *O* is for objective information, including your daily exams and lab findings, the *A* is for your assessment based on the subjective and objective findings, and finally, the *P* is for your plan for the patient. Is that clear, Mr. Maizel? If not, you may want to ask Mr. Zuri. He seems to have a good handle on things."

"Yes, it's very clear, Dr. Jones."

Dr. Jones nodded. "Have a pleasant evening, and I will see you bright and early for morning rounds. At that time, I want to hear a quantification of her weight loss; what current medications she is on; and a complete, detailed summary of her social, family, and past medical histories. Be prepared, Mr. Maizel! That is not a suggestion. That is a demand. Failure of preparation will elicit certain consequences. Is that clear, Mr. Maizel?"

Dr. Jones walked away, and then abruptly stopped. Without turning around, he said, "By the way, Ms. Dixon's skin appears quite icteric, not slightly jaundiced as you depicted in your presentation. In fact, her sclera is yellowed, as well as the base of her tongue. All are findings that some significant hepatic insult is in play, Mr. Maizel. Whether this is a complete failure of the liver or a temporary inflammation from an infection, it requires a thorough investigation. I need you to take this seriously and contemplate what this means when you do your reading tonight! That is important to note. I would make sure you follow her liver enzymes, so make sure to check her SGOT, SGPT, and alkaline phosphatase, and get a total bilirubin and get them serially over the next few days. You need to investigate that liver more."

He then continued sauntering down the long hallway.

Damn, did he examine her, too? That man is way ahead of me!

As Jack made his way back to the on-call room on the second floor, he took the elevators down to the third floor and took a short-cut through the pediatric ward. A variety of child sounds—laughing, giggling, crying, and screaming—filled the hallways. He always took the back stairs located at the end of the pediatric wing that led directly down to the on-call quarters on the second floor. He found solace going that way and always looked forward to seeing the nurses happy and smiling while some of the not-so-sick kids were playing. It always made him feel better after a rough day.

*   *   *

Jack needed to get a few minutes of shut-eye before his call duties started in about an hour. He lay down on the bunk bed, feeling inept and miserable about his encounter with Dr. Jones. *What the hell did I get myself into? Why am I in medical school?*

As he dozed off, the pager sounded, and Jack was commanded to come to the emergency room for a hospital admission. Sitting up in bed, he hung his head for a minute, clearing it. *Dr. Jones is trying to break me, my parents don't care about my happiness, and I hate all this*, he thought. Jack began to cry from fatigue and frustration. After a few minutes, he got up to splash cold water against his face and then made his way down to the ER.

16

After two sets of difficult back-to-back hospital admissions through the emergency room, Jack Maizel finished writing orders and even drew their lab work. Once they got to their hospital rooms, Jack did an EKG reading on one patient and placed a nasogastric tube in another.

He finally got back to the on-call room a little before 2 a.m. and fell asleep right after throwing himself on the bed.

The tone and voice pager abruptly blasted several short but loud beeps before a voice replaced the reverberations: "Pager 377, call Six North nurses' station at extension 4175. Extension 4175, extension 4175."

In the dark call room, he reached over to grab his Motorola Pageboy and silence it with the top button, then looked at his watch to see that it was only a few minutes after two.

A bit disoriented and tired, he didn't want to deal with another patient just now. As he drifted back to sleep, Jack's mind floated back to his earlier thoughts: *What am I doing here? Why am I doing this? I hate every minute of med school and don't want to deal with sick people. This just isn't my thing. Who cares about being rich? I don't need it. What if my folks disinherit me? I don't even want their money! Not worth it! My parents want this, not me! It's my life, right?* After another moment, as the sleepiness hung over him, he thought, *I need to light up a joint right now!*

Without warning, the pager went off again: "Call Six North nursing desk at extension 4175. 4175. 4175. That's Six North nurs—"

Jack turned off the pager and roughly grabbed the phone. Two rings into the call, a calm and gentle female voice answered and said, "Six North, this is Sandy speaking."

"Dr. Maizel here . . . what do you people want?"

"Oh, hi, Jack! Your patient in six-two-eight, Miss Dixon, is complaining of a bad headache, and she doesn't have any aspirin or Tylenol ordered. Her blood pressure is a little bit up. Could you come up to evaluate her please?"

Jack blew a deep breath into the phone and raised his voice. "Are you kidding? Just give her some fricking Tylenol, and I'll see her in the morning!"

"Yes, but her blood pressure is at one thirty-nine over ninety-four, and she is complaining of a little bit of nausea, too."

"That BP is okay. Nothing wrong with that! Give her some Tylenol like I said and tell her to go to sleep!"

The nurse persisted. "Her pressure is much higher than her admission BP, and I would feel better if she was at least looked at by someone. Even you, Jack!"

"'Even you'! What's that supposed to mean? I'm her doctor, and I'll take a look at her in the morning."

"Jack, Miss Dixon doesn't feel very well. We don't know what her problems are, but I'm worried about the blood pressure, the headache, and now the nausea. If you don't come up, I'll call Dr. Jones, and he'll make sure to fix things! I think he'll even try to fix you!"

"You people are just sitting on your big fat heinies and thinking of ways to agitate us doctors. That's all this is about! Do you think I'm that stupid?"

"No, Jack, you're not stupid at all! But you're not a doctor yet, either!"

Jack was upset that he had to get out of bed—after just getting into bed. He exaggerated a deep sigh into the phone. "Fine!" Then he slammed the phone on its cradle. *These nurses are crazy!*

17

Without knocking, Jack Maizel pushed the door open, flicked the overhead fluorescent lights on, and entered Mildred Dixon's hospital room. He knew he was out of control and knew that if this got back to Dr. Jones, he'd catch hell from him, but he was upset about being called out of bed for something he thought was trivial. Still, he knew he had to be cautious about Dr. Jones.

"So, what's up, Dixon?"

Under the covers, half asleep, she responded, "Well if it isn't Sonny Boy! What brings you here to see me at this hour?"

"What the hell, Dixon? You're supposed to be sick. At least that's what the nurses tell me. I have to check you over to make sure you ain't faking it!"

"Why would I pretend being sick? I'm in a hospital where sick people stay, right? So, deductive reasoning, as they say, tells everyone that I have some sort of ailment. Why would you even think I am making anything up?"

"Look, Dixon, don't get smart with me. I'm your doctor, so you need to tell me what's wrong with you. Be straight with me, all right? I could be sound asleep if it weren't for you!"

Mildred Dixon, with increasing moisture in her eyes, looked at the young medical student. "Please tell me, Sonny Boy," she said softly, "why are you always so cross and nasty to others? You always seem wetter than a wet hen. Why? Especially to me. I never did anything wrong or bad to you. What did anyone ever do to you to make you act this way? There must be something seriously wrong with you—"

"I don't need to take this from you or anyone else. I can just walk out anytime I want to. You can just continue to suffer from your headaches!"

Mildred felt her blood rushing to her face as her anger rose to a boiling point. In a strong and firm voice, she declared, "I'm fixin' to have a hissy fit with you, Sonny Boy! I am tired of you." She looked at him cold and hard. "That's always your answer, isn't it, Sonny Boy? Just walk out. Well, don't rush out on my account. Just go. Walk away! Throw other people away if they give you any trouble at all. That's cowardly and you know it! You probably have a history of turning your back to people and whatever comes up that you can't deal with. That's ugly and you know it. So, quit being ugly, Sonny Boy!

"You remind me of little boys who just can't cope with things. They get so mad about something and don't have the words to get out their frustrations, so they just simply walk out or scream and carry on with a tantrum. You need to face bad things in your life, accept defeats and losses, and deal with difficult people. It's the bad things in life that make you strong and teach you to understand life! If you don't learn these things, you will never be at peace with yourself. You will never live a happy life!"

Mildred paused for a moment while Jack just stood there, a bit stunned. He had never been spoken to this way by a patient or anyone else, not even by his parents. He always had control, and he was always the boss between himself and any patients or anyone—except for his parents or Dr. Jones, of course.

"Men in my days weren't sissy men like you," Mildred said, fuming. "They would never bully a woman, let alone a woman who's old enough to be your grandma! Not in a million years would they ever yell at anyone—woman, child, or the old. They had discipline, son. That's something missing in your life, Sonny Boy! And, you know what else is wrong with you? Responsibility! You don't have any responsibility to be nice and caring! I think your problem is that you had no adversities in your life. Nothing bad ever happened to you. I think you've been pampered like a baby all your life, and nobody set you straight.

"Upon my word, Sonny Boy, your problem is that you came from one of those rich families, and you always had everything you wanted. Sure, you may be rich and smart, but you have no worth in your life. You have no purpose because you're not passionate about anything. You are empty! Your heart and soul are a shell with no substance. You're like a beautifully wrapped Christmas gift with a nice bow, but when you open it up, there's nothing inside it except for maybe a lump of coal like what Charlie Brown got! That's you, Sonny Boy. You are just a shell without any meat inside. I feel sorry for you because you are what they call a *Loser*, spelled with a capital *L*! Now do what you need to do and then please leave."

Jack, taken aback, didn't know what to say. "What are you, some kind of a psychiatrist?" he asked, in a gentler voice.

"Why, yes! I already told you about that part of my life when you came back after your boss yelled at you for not asking me about my life. You didn't think I knew why you came back, did you? But it was clear to this old nurse. I've been around, Sonny Boy.

"I told you when you came back to interview me, yesterday, I was a psyche nurse and later a behavioral health counselor for over thirty years at Kentucky State Hospital until I retired two years ago. You don't have good listening manners, and you were upset 'cause you got in trouble. I'm not surprised you don't remember! That's not a good characteristic to have as a doctor, Sonny Boy!

"State, as we called it back then, was an asylum. Perhaps you know about that place. It's where no one wants to go either as a medical person or a patient. Hardly anyone ever leaves there, either. Kinda like that song. Oh, I can't recall who sang it—some musical group named after a bird. The Hawks or maybe The Vultures, I think. But it's a song about some California hotel—you know up in one of those western states—where people can't ever leave!"

"Look, Miss Dixon, I can't remember everything! I gotta say, you are the one who will never leave here if you don't start working with me!" *That was reactionary!* thought Jack. *What an ass I am to be sarcastic like that! I need to take a breath and slow down! Did I just call her "miss"?*

Jack breathed in deeply. "Okay . . . look, I apologize. I'm just tired, and I shouldn't have said what I said or spoken to you in that tone of voice. Let's start over, okay? The floor nurse called me and said that you had a headache and were sick to your stomach. Is that right? She also told me that your blood pressure was a little elevated. I want to look you over, and we'll go from there, okay?"

"Goodness gracious, Sonny Boy, I'm surprised you can speak in a decent tone of voice and act a bit civilized toward me. I'll say I'm a little impressed—maybe you do have some manners hidden in there somewhere. But I'll tell you something . . . I still won't change my mind about you! You're still nothing but a spoiled Sonny Boy to me!"

*   *   *

As he performed a neuro exam to rule out any neurological causes for the headaches, Mildred was attentive and listened to his commands.

"Okay, now look up. Look down. Good. Now sideways," he instructed as he used a penlight to watch her eye movements. "I'm going to look at the back of your eyes now with this otoscope, so I'm dimming the room lights a bit. Don't look directly at my scope light when I bring it nearer to your eyes. I'm going to come in from an angle but just keep staring straight ahead of you. Good job, Dixon!"

"Sonny Boy, you do remember that I was educated as a nurse, right? So that means I do know the procedures for an eye exam. I'm not saying this to be arrogant or a know-it-all, but I do want to commend you, that you are doing a good job." She smiled. "You even show that you have a little heart. Funny, but you remind me of my Bert in some ways."

Jack, contemplating his conversation with Miss Dixon as he gathered his equipment, kept quiet. He was bothered by what this woman said to him about not having passion and purpose. She also said there was something missing in his life. It hit home for him: *I don't have passion or purpose for anything I do. Why? But don't I? I loved Ajax. She was mine and how I spent so much time teaching her all those jumps and how to posture up just right to be a champion! A champion equestrian. We were a great team. Yup, I was passionate about her and—*

"Excuse me, Sonny Boy? Are you okay? You look like you are in some kind of a trance."

"Sure, Dixon!" He caught himself. "Oops, I'm sorry. I'm trying hard to call you *miss*, but I like calling you Dixon. It's kinda endearing to me for some reason. I want to be nice and ask if I may continue to call you Dixon and you can keep calling me Sonny Boy."

"Okay, that's a deal, Sonny Boy. Hey, if they can call Nixon 'Nixon,' then I guess why not just call me Dixon!"

*   *   *

"So, who exactly is Bert to you?" Jack asked while he was writing his chart notes.

"He's my lifelong sweetheart. What a man he is! He's a man's man. Polite, sincere, kind, masculine, a take-charge kind of guy, and a powerful man! He's like what a real man should be." She was beaming with a broad smile as she looked up toward the ceiling. "I must tell you he always makes me as happy as a boardinghouse pup, Sonny Boy! He's sweeter than stolen honey, and the man fulfills my inner being!"

"You told me you weren't married, Dixon."

"I'm not," she replied. "You don't have to be married to have a sweetheart, Sonny Boy. You certainly do have a lot of growing up to do, don't you?"

"So, you're saying that you've had a boyfriend for all of your life, lifelong as you say, but you never married him?"

"Bingo!" She put both hands to her cheeks, feigning surprise. "Oh my, you are quite a genius, Sonny Boy!"

Just then, the voice pager went off: "Code five hundred in the ER STAT! Code five hundred in the ER STAT!"

"Oh my," Mildred exclaimed. "You better get going!"

Jack Maizel, without saying a word, rushed out of the room with intent and focus in his eyes.

18

Jack Maizel happened to be the first medical student to arrive in the emergency room. To his surprise, there were no physicians in the department. But, without hesitation, Jack immediately made his way to where the security guard was pointing.

"What's going on?" he asked the nurse, rushing toward where other personnel were making their way.

"Gunshot victim brought in by civilian personnel! Transported via private auto. He's unresponsive in bay four. No doctors yet!"

Jack rushed into the bay. There was one nurse doing CPR on a recumbent man on a gurney with bloodied sheets. Another nurse was putting monitor electrode leads to his chest to check for vital signs.

"Do we have a pulse?" Jack quickly asked.

"Yes, I just got his heart going!" replied the nurse who stopped doing compressions.

"His respiratory rates are shallow. Get me an Ambu bag now!" Jack said. "I need to intubate and get an airway going. Someone get me an ET tube—STAT! Get started on an IV on this man, too."

After intubating him and starting the IV lactated ringers' solution, Jack could take a quick breather and now do a full assessment.

The ER attending physician, Dr. Julie Sims, arrived just a few seconds later along with other nursing personnel. "I'll take over now," said Dr. Sims. Without looking at Jack, as she was focused on the patient, she asked, "Give me a report."

Just then, one of the nurses said, "I got a quick history from the parents who transported him in their car. He is a seventeen-year-old male who was found in the parents' detached garage after a loud bang noise. The father found him unresponsive with a gun lying next to him."

"When I arrived, he had a faint pulse and shallow breathing," added Jack. "So I intubated him and started IV lactated ringers. I was just doing my assessment when you walked in."

The nurses were cleaning him up and resecuring the IV needle in his left arm and the endotracheal tube around his mouth. There was a gunshot wound to the right side of his head with blood caked over his hair and face and down to the upper parts of his body. Large pieces of brain matter were missing at the bullet's exit point on the left side of his head. *How is he even alive?* thought Jack.

"Where's his NG tube?" asked Dr. Sims.

"His nose, as you can see, is pretty far damaged due to the blood and the entry wound—looks like something smacked his face or he fell on it—so I didn't want to try the nasogastric tube," said Jack. "I was just going to insert it through his oral cavity while we have an oral airway device inserted."

"Great, then do it now! We don't want him to aspirate, do we?"

The ER physician examined both the entry and exit wounds, when suddenly the monitors started flashing and alarming. Jack immediately began CPR and the ER physician grabbed the defibrillator paddles and ordered everyone to stand clear as she tried to shock the man's heart into beating on its own.

Making every attempt to save his life, Dr. Sims, after noting that the pupils were fixed and dilated with no heart rate and no respiratory efforts, pronounced the man deceased.

In the meantime, a young girl in the family counseling room, a few doors down from bay 4, was screaming at the boy's parents. In near hysteria, she was alleging that his parents murdered her boyfriend because they didn't like her. "What did you do to our son that made him want to shoot himself?" the parents yelled at the girl.

The girl screamed, "Why did you shoot him? You are murderers!"

Jack approached the three people in the room. All were crying, and the girl continued to yell. Jack said, "I'm Dr. Maizel, and I need everyone to remain calm, please. I assume you are the parents," he said as he pointed to the couple. "And you are a girlfriend?"

They all nodded.

"I understand this is a difficult situation. We don't know what led to this, and I assume you don't, either. So please don't make accusations and suppositions. The police will help you sort this. I am sorry to report that he has passed away."

They all started sobbing loudly. Hospital social workers arrived to attempt comfort and support. The boy's mother reached over to Jack and gave him a hug. "We knew this was going to happen. It was just a matter of time. It's because of this slut, here."

"You're a whore and your husband's a pimp!" the girl shot back. "That's why Will killed himself! He couldn't stand either one of you, and he told me many times he'd rather be dead than to spend his life knowing you two had something to do with his life!"

Jack, staying unusually calm, said, "Please, I ask that you refrain from accusations. That's harsh, and there is no need for that here."

He asked one of the social workers to take the girl to another room as he escorted the parents to another. After Jack spent about half an hour with the parents, Dr. Sims came in, expressed condolences, and asked Jack to come with her. The police had arrived and wanted to question them.

Before Jack left, the father stood up and shook his hand and said, "Thank you, Doctor. We appreciated your calmness and levelheadedness. You're a fine man, sir!"

When they were alone, Dr. Sims said, "Maizel, good job in there. You did your best to stabilize basically a DOA. Amazing job intubating and getting that IV in. I appreciate you taking charge when I couldn't get there in time! Thanks! I'll let your attending know!"

After being interviewed by the police, Jack left to go back up to the on-call room, feeling good about himself but bad for the seventeen-year-old and the true victims—the parents and his girlfriend. He was surprised how calm the situation made him and how levelheaded he felt during the entire ordeal. He'd never overseen an intensely stressful situation where life-and-death matters were at stake.

Maybe I am okay as a doctor, Jack thought.

19

"Well, you certainly got here bright and early this morning."

"It was a rough night, and I never got any sleep—again, Dixon," said Jack, looking very fatigued. "I went to the emergency room when I left you, and they had a self-inflected gunshot victim that I had to help with. He was just a kid—seventeen years old! It was a nightmare, Dixon. No one should have to see something horrible like that!"

Mildred Dixon could see that the medical student was quite exasperated by this event. She wanted to be compassionate. "I'm sorry to hear that. So, what happened? Did he die?"

"What do you think? The parents and the girlfriend of the victim started carrying on while we were taking life-saving measures for the boy. They were angry and yelling at each other. Parents accusing the girlfriend and the girlfriend accusing the parents. It was a mess, Dixon. In the meantime, the poor boy died. Then, as if it wasn't bad enough, the boy's girlfriend starts screaming at the top of her lungs and uses profanity at the boy's parents, accusing them of murder!"

Jack rubbed his weary face. "It was just a crazy night, Dixon. A short time later, just after things got settled down and I was on my way to the on-call quarters, one of the second-year internal medicine residents, in the middle of all that, got into a fight with another patient he was examining. It seems that the patient kept demanding more pain pills from him and started shoving the resident doctor. He got mad—couldn't take it anymore—and jumped on the gurney where the patient was propped up and started punching him in the face! It took a few of us to get him off the dang patient! Then, guess what happened to the doctor? The police came and arrested him for assault and battery and took him out in handcuffs!"

Jack Maizel shook his head and rubbed his face some more.

Not knowing how to react and wanting to change the morbid subject, Mildred said, "My Bert knows what to do in these situations. He's a very tough man, but he also has such a passionate side for everyone. He's like a genius when it comes to handling people. I think he would make a good doctor if he was younger. He's so patient."

"Oh, yeah, Bert! Almost forgot about him! The mystery *lover* who just crept out of nowhere!" exclaimed Jack. "Who the heck is he, Dixon? I don't believe that he's been your boyfriend forever. You know the saying 'either shit or get off the pot'? He can't still be your boyfriend. Either he married you or dumped you! Which is it? And, if the guy is that important to you, how come you didn't tell me about him during my history interviews with you? What the heck happened to him, Dixon?"

Mildred looked down toward the floor while she sat on the side of her hospital bed, her feet dangling.

"My Bert was in the war—World War II—and suffered some bad injuries. He lost an arm, and his face was badly disfigured. He was captured and was put in one of those Stalag prison camps. His mind wasn't ever the same, either. When he came back from Europe, he barely could face me. He kept telling me that I deserved better. He broke off our engagement and said he had a bad case of battle shock and that he would probably be dangerous around people. I thought he went over the deep end until I started reading about it. Just about the time I retired from Kentucky State Hospital, they came up with the term PTSD to describe people like Bert. That means post-traumatic stress disorder, if you never heard of it."

She played with the necklace around her neck. "The sad thing about it all is, I didn't care what he looked like. I loved Bert. Still do. That's why I still call him my boyfriend. I didn't love him any less because of the way he looked. If he had lost both legs and both arms and an eyeball, it didn't matter to me. I loved him before he left for the war and even more when he came back. I was in love with First Lieutenant Bert Vines and not his body parts, for God's sake!"

Jack Maizel, mesmerized by Mildred's passion, continued to sit in silence listening to her story. Then he asked, "So, where is Bert now?"

"He wouldn't marry me even though I was so much in love with him. I saw him once after he came back from the war, but he did everything he could to avoid me. Oh, Sonny Boy! Life is so unfair sometimes. Why did he forsake me? I have never gotten over him, and he remains in my heart to this day. This moment. Our souls always blended with each other."

"Okay but where is he now? You're saying that you haven't seen him for a long time, but you consider him your boyfriend?"

"I don't know where he is. But I want to see him. I want to touch my Bert!"

A small tear suddenly appeared from Jack's right eye, but he quickly blinked it away, stunned by this emotional revelation. He was suddenly speechless. Not knowing what to say or do, he finally got up and said, "Let me do my daily exam on you so I can chart it. My friend Ahgri Zuri is coming in to take the rest of my Saturday call soon, but I'll be back tomorrow morning. I have to go to an important party for my mother. She's kinda like a local socialite and likes to show off her racehorses, house, and herself. She even likes showing me off. Always telling her friends that I'm her doctor son and that I'm going to be this great plastic surgeon in town. I play along, but this is what I think about that." He pointed an index finger toward his open mouth and feigned a gagging episode.

"I'm going to try to sneak off and get some rest in the middle of that gaudy party."

"Maybe you can play with some of those racehorses instead of wasting your time on being at a party," said Mildred, coming out of her haze. "They sure are pretty. I always wanted to ride one. So, your mom owns racehorses?"

Jack, taken aback a bit, replied, "Yes, they are pretty. I used to have one of my own when I was a kid. It wasn't a racehorse but an Appaloosa. An Appaloosa I taught dressage techniques to."

"Oh, do you still ride and have him?"

Jack's mood dampened a bit, and he quietly replied, "She was a mare and she died. I need to get going, Dixon. I'll tell you about Ajax next time I see you, okay? Ahgri will take good care of you! See you!"

With that he rushed out, head hung low.

20

The early September day was unseasonably warm. Although the day was approaching evening, the sun's intensity still penetrated deeply into the crowd of people gathered at the Burk-Grayson Annual Bourbon and Horseshoe Soiree.

The event began forty-eight years ago with stepbrothers Franklin P. Burk and Henry Tyler Grayson and became an annual fixture among the rich and elite. During the early years, family members and the area's wealthy horse farm owners attended. These days, the gala attracted hundreds of dignitaries from all around the Commonwealth of Kentucky, including the political elite, university presidents, local athletes, famous Kentucky actors who made it big on the silver screen, and even friends and foes of the Maizel family. The annual gathering always turned this rural area into a small municipality.

Workers rushed here and there to make sure the event went off properly and perfectly. Most were red-faced with beads of sweat lining their foreheads, and all were fatigued by the draining heat. It didn't help that they were required to wear mandatory Kentucky jodhpurs with black riding boots and red coats that elevated their core body temperatures. Every year, at least two or three of these unfortunate workers would pass out from heat exhaustion and could not complete the evening chores.

The magnificent white pillared mansion, surrounded by lush emerald-green rolling acres, was located a half mile from the main entrance road off Newtown Pike. Strikingly shaped and well-manicured magnolia trees, some still holding on to their flowers, lined the long and winding drive that led up to the splendid manor. Arriving guests could hear the chamber orchestra serenading them as they neared the grand house.

The complex was so large that the grounds could accommodate hundreds of guests at any given time without a hint of overcrowding. Japanese paper lanterns were strung all around the property, outlining the property like a giant umbrella. Makeshift and smaller water features were located throughout the grounds, and incredible floral arrangements were everywhere, scenting the air with sweet fragrances.

An army of attendants stood at attention in the front promenade between the mansion and a huge fountain that greeted visitors. Most of these escorts were trim and muscular male high school and well-known college athletes from local schools. They wore smartly tailored turquoise-blue suits, swanky fedoras, and white gloves as they eagerly awaited their guests. Upon a car's arrival, a team of attendants immediately opened the door and helped attendees out, taking extra precautions to prevent falls or accidents. A warm welcome and a smile were bestowed on each guest, and then they were escorted to the main grounds and formally introduced through a loudspeaker.

Oddly, in addition to all the pomp of the massive property, professional jockeys donning colorful silks rode perfectly muscled Thoroughbred horses and sauntered among the partygoers, sipping mint juleps, as if they were also invited guests.

This was Jack Maizel's twenty-sixth over-the-top party. Although he did not remember much of the first five, he knew he hadn't liked any since the time he became aware of these events.

As a toddler, his mom dressed him in a tuxedo, and today was no different. The bow tie was strangling, droplets of sweat rolled off his head, and he was tremendously thirsty. He had no idea who most of these people were—nor did he care. People came up to him and grasped his hand with clammy fingers and shook it. Unknown women gave him hugs and kiss-pecks on his cheeks, forehead, and even on the lips. One seemingly inebriated elderly lady even patted his behind, then had the nerve to grasp a buttock cheek. "He's got strong meat on them there bones!" she squealed in delight.

Everyone laughed, but it was embarrassing to be the center of a joke.

He watched his parents, who appeared to be in their element. He could not help but marvel at their hypocrisy. They didn't like most of these people—they always talked bad about them—but they spent lots of money to entertain, laugh, and socialize with them. His mom, Elizabeth Burk-Maizel, was an original Burk bloodline. Many years of gene training, Jack decided, had made her an expert at maneuvering between guests and being a hospitable hostess. She seemed to know who to talk with, when to talk, and who to introduce to whom. *If only they could see her bad side*, he thought.

Dad married into money. He was a poor medical student and an even poorer medical resident but hit pay dirt when he took care of Jack's mom's dad, who had severe heart issues. His parents met, fell in love, and got married. It wasn't that they were really in love—emotionally—but they were in love with the convenience of their social status by having each other. Jack's mom was rich, so his dad would become rich. His mom wanted a man with a title. What better than to be able to flaunt his name—"Oh, yes, my husband, Dr. Peter Maizel, certainly you know him. A very famous cardiovascular surgeon who saves lives every day!"

Jack's dad immediately fit right into elite society. Amazingly, he had the gift of gab and could hold court to a bunch of monkeys, and they would pay attention to him and probably even laugh at his jokes.

"Jack!" A loud voice startled him. It took a second, but he cringed as he realized the voice belonged to his mother.

"Why aren't you mingling with our guests? Goodness gracious! I am so ashamed to tell people you are my son! You have an ass and a mouth, so use it to propel those legs of yours and talk to our guests. Make them happy that they are at this grand event. Don't you understand that they want to congregate with you? Tell them about medical school and all the people's lives you saved. Look alive, son!"

A sudden intrusion by his mom always created anxiety for him. This was a pattern for most of his life. Attention was given to him only when there was a crisis or when his mother wanted—no—demanded that he act or do things in a certain manner according to her standards.

"I'm tired, Mother, and have no interest in mingling. I was on call the past few days and just don't care to socialize—"

"I don't want to hear any of that crap, Jack Burk-Maizel! This is the most important thing you do this year and every year. You need to act like a Burk and be a Burk! For God's sake, you are a Burk! Now, get out there and talk with someone!"

When Jack hesitated, she proclaimed, "Now, mister, not tomorrow!"

Jack, already in a foul mood, replied, "If I don't, you're going to put me out to pasture or shoot me like you did Ajax, right? Oh, sorry, my mistake, the proper term is *destroy*, isn't it? That's what you always do when people or animals don't follow your bossy commands. You just toss them aside."

She maintained her composure and, still smiling, replied, "Jack, enough of that! There are people here, and they listen to everything. Just get out there and talk to people. Come on, sweetheart, make your momma proud!"

"Let's face it, Mother! I am nothing but a charm on a bracelet for you. You have lots of them—your distinguished name, your mansion, your racehorses, your money, your employees. It goes on and on. Oh, yeah, let's not forget you doctor husband, and now you have me being a doctor son! You have completed the perfect accessories for yourself!

"Let me tell you, Mother, I don't want to be another one of your trinkets, dangling from a golden bracelet that you flaunt in front of others. I am Jack, and I want to be myself—not someone's doctor son!"

She tried to smile but now was having more difficulties hiding her grimaces. It was embarrassing, and she did not handle embarrassment well.

Suddenly turning around and putting her hand against a man's back, she instantly recognized him as the lieutenant governor of Kentucky and said in an exaggerated Southern belle drawl, "Oh, Steward, my dear, how are you? It's been too long since we last spoke. Why, you look more handsome now than when I first met you all those years ago in high school. Oh, please let me introduce you to my son, the future Dr. Jack Burk-Maizel!"

Jack did not say anything. Once again, another sweaty palm came out to grab his hand and shake it vigorously up and down.

* * *

After a bugler bellowed out "Call to Post" and the chamber orchestra played a jazzy rendition of Kentucky's state song, dinner was served in the main dining hall of the mansion. Each guest was personally escorted by the smartly dressed attendants wearing those fancy fedora hats.

Jack sat at the host's table with the governor and the president of the largest university in the state.

The governor rose to make a toast. "Here's to another phenomenal annual event put on by the Burk-Maizel family. Famously, as we all know, the Burk-Grayson dynasty was started by the late stepbrothers Henry Tyler Grayson and Franklin P. Burk—both were gentlemen extraordinaire, and now Franklin's daughter, the most beautiful Elizabeth Burk-Maizel, and her husband, Dr. Peter Maizel, head this amazing empire. Such excellent people and outstanding hosts. Here's to the Burk-Maizel family!"

Jack, a bit inebriated, immediately rose when the governor completed his toast. He raised his champaign glass above his head and said, "And that Franklin Burk was a real asshole and so am I!" He snickered. "Elizabeth programmed me to be that way—a real Burk! And let me tell you a story—"

The orchestra started before he could finish, and his mother got up, patted Jack's back, smiled, and gave him a kiss on his cheek as if this was all part of the festivities. "He's such a ham sometimes!" she said, laughing.

Jack had a few bites as he sat with the governor's entourage. Mostly keeping quiet after the outburst, he listened to the politicians' derogatory opinions of their political opponents and how their rivals would destroy the Commonwealth if they ever got into office. As the meals were consumed and the drinking took over, the political affronts exploded, and vulgarity overtook many of the conversations around each table.

With Jack imbibing heavily, his filters faded even more, and he began to argue with those around the table. His mother, a bit on edge and seeing the commotion, quickly intervened and got her assistants to isolate Jack by coaxing him away. Eventually, they led him to his third-floor childhood bedroom and locked the room. He knew the routine. They would always do that to him whenever he was out of control and didn't comply with his mother's expectations and demands.

The psychology counselors used to tell his mom that the lockup routine was dangerous for a child's proper upbringing and may lead to mental anguish and acting out. She always argued with them, telling them that this was the way the Burks handled their problems—directly and without mercy! "You do something wrong, and you will pay for it," she would say. "This will avoid further problems down the road!"

As Jack did many times during his youth, he yelled out: "Don't lock me up here! I'm not Rapunzel! I have brown hair, not golden!" Then he smiled a wicked smile. He had a secret that only he and one other person—the child psychologist who helped him many times—knew. He had a key to his room and could get out anytime. He'd used it before, but this time, he decided not to, as he did not want to go back to the party. He took a few more sips of bourbon and a few puffs from the weed he had stashed in a box under his bed.

Jack finally tired out and went to lie down. He stared at the walls adorned with photos of him and his Appaloosa, Ajax. So many medals and trophies they won for their dressage events. He was proud of their accomplishments. Then, he began to cry. Intense and vigorous at first, it simmered down to sobs as he fell asleep. Jack knew he had to be up in a few hours to make his morning rounds at the hospital.

21

"*Shikamoo*!" exclaimed the man as he entered room 628. A warm smile and a gentle handshake greeted Mildred as he said, "Do you remember me from your first night here?"

"*Salama*!" replied Mildred Dixon. "*Za jioni*, Ahgri Zuri!" Mildred had a perfect Swahili accent. "Yes, of course I remember you. You were the nice student who took care of me while that other one just walked out because he was in such a bad mood."

Ahgri Zuri stopped, surprised by her immediate and fluid response in Swahili. After regaining composure, he asked, "Miss Mildred, may I ask how do you understand and speak Swahili so well? I remember telling you to sleep well in Swahili, as a joke when I first saw you on your first night here. And now! Now, you can suddenly speak in my native Swahili language. How can this be, miss?"

Mildred chuckled. "I thought you might be surprised by this. I've been waiting for you to visit so that I could show off my language skills! I am self-taught because I always wanted to travel to East Africa and visit some of the countries, especially around the Kenya and Tanganyika area. Oh, how I reflect on all those animals—so many different kinds just roaming on the plains being free and happy!"

She put her hand to her mouth as if she made a mistake and appeared startled by an error she just made. "Oops, I'm sorry. Your country was known as Tanganyika when I was younger. Now I know it as Tanzania!" She spoke with a schoolgirl's enthusiasm. "I am in heaven when I can learn new things, especially different languages. I had a friend long ago who taught himself how to read, write, and speak in seven different languages, mainly because he wanted to read the different interpretations of the Bible to make sure he didn't miss anything through translations. That was impressive to me, and that's what got me inspired to study languages."

"Oh my. I must say, that is quite impressive, Ms. Dixon. It is certainly music to my humble ears. I am astonished that someone who hails from rural eastern Kentucky knows what Swahili is, let alone understands some of it. You even know the contraction of saying good evening—just like us natives. For example, you did not even apply the word *habari* before *za*. Most non-natives say, '*Habari za asabuhi*,' or '*Habari za jioni*' to do our greetings of good morning or good evening. You know to just say '*za jioni*' like native speakers do so often. You are quite extraordinary, my dear lady."

Mildred replied, "I didn't live in eastern Kentucky all my life, Ahgri! I grew up in the city just on the outskirts of Louisville. A big metropolitan area, even back then. Right after nursing school at Norton Memorial Infirmary, I went to take special training at Bowman Field as a flight nurse specializing in nursing triage evacuation by air. That was during the World War II years, around 1942 and 1943. Oh, what an exciting time of my life that was!

"Bowman Field, a rinky-dink airport just outside of Louisville, got to be known as Air Base City during World War II, as it became the busiest airport in the country because of the influx of airmen and nurses training there. I later served in the Army Air Forces overseas, and when I got back home, I eventually made my way to the Lexington area. I got interested in combat exhaustion disorders because I saw a lot of young men's minds and emotions ruined by combat. Later, I became a psychiatric nurse at Eastern State Hospital, here in Lexington, until I retired a couple of years ago.

"Believe me, I don't know the Swahili language well—just enough to be dangerous, as they say. I do have a keen interest in etymology though—especially with surnames—you know, like what people's names mean. How and where did they originate? I think it is interesting that many times the meaning of last names fits people's personalities so well. For example, your last name, Zuri. I know in Swahili this means 'beautiful'! It fits you perfectly!"

She looked at him expectantly.

"Miss Dixon, you are too much," said Ahgri. "If you hailed from the Chagga tribe—the people of my father—I would honor you with the name *Mrembo wa Ajabu*. This means 'remarkably beautiful.' And so you are, miss!"

She giggled and thanked him. "You know, your friend's last name, Maizel, is mostly a German-derived name and seems to be common in the Jewish heritage. It means 'little mouse' in German and Yiddish." She giggled again, covering her mouth with her hands.

"And I thought it meant 'big ugly rat,'" said Ahgri. He laughed loudly, and Mildred joined in, clapping her hands enthusiastically.

They shared small talk for a while longer, and then Ahgri asked whether she needed anything for the evening before he left.

"Yes, there is one more thing. Could you tell me your story, Ahgri? What are you doing here?"

Ahgri looked contemplatively at her. "What do you mean, Miss Mildred?"

"Why are you in Kentucky? Where are your parents? How did you learn to speak English? Does being a black man in the middle of a very white community like Lexington bother you? There are so many questions I'm not sure where to begin."

Ahgri Zuri sat down and relaxed his posture. "Oh, Miss Dixon, I fear that I would be here all night if I told you my life's story. It is somewhat complicated, and I am not the typical African man. But, since you asked, I will give you the—how do you say it—the *Reader's Digest* version of my life's tale."

Just then, a knock on the door startled them both. Ahgri began walking to the door when Dr. Jones and a young woman walked in.

Dr. Jones extended his hand to Mildred. "Good Saturday evening to you, Miss Dixon." He glanced toward Ahgri Zuri and gave a subtle nod. "Mr. Zuri." He looked back at Mildred and smiled. "Miss Dixon, I'm Dr. William Jones, the attending physician for the internal medicine services this month. This is Miss Annie Chang, RN, and she is assisting me today."

"So pleased to meet you, Doctor, and you, too, Miss Chang." She looked at Dr. Jones. "I heard you during your morning rounds outside my door with all those students. I liked it when you let Sonny Boy have it. It was as funny as all get-out! He sure does think a lot of himself, doesn't he? Where I come from, we would say he's too big for his britches!"

Everyone laughed.

"But, somehow, I see a lot of good in Sonny Boy. There's something deep down in his soul that is missing, I think."

Dr. Jones smiled and asked, "Sonny Boy?"

"Oh, I gave him that nickname because he reminds me of a little boy. A mischievous little boy who runs around pulling on little girls' hair but continues to act like a big shot in front of his friends."

Dr. Jones laughed. "Fits him to a *T*! Yes, somewhere under the façade of his outward character, I think he's got a lot of good in him, but he certainly needs to grow up a bit to be a good doctor. My job is to see to it that he gets that way. Thanks for caring, Miss Dixon.

"I saw you in passing the other night when you were admitted. Although I did not have a chance to speak with you then, I want to formally welcome you now. I know this sounds odd—that someone is welcoming you to a hospital—but I want you to know that we care about you and will make sure to take the best care of all your health needs." Dr. Jones paused. "I do know quite a bit about your medical history already. We are still awaiting several preliminary tests, so we do not know exactly what's wrong with you yet."

"Do you have a preliminary diagnosis yet, Doctor? I'm a former psychiatric nurse at Eastern State Hospital, so I do understand some medical lingo."

"I don't want to say too much yet. But I have always been direct and truthful to my patients, no matter how bad the news. So, I will tell you that I worry about a form of cancer with you. Specifically, I'm looking at pancreatic cancer. It could be other things as well, such as hepatitis—non-A, non-B. We just don't know at this time. But please don't jump to conclusions just yet. You are in good hands with Mr. Zuri, here, and, of course, Mr. Maizel. They work directly with me, and I will be with you one hundred percent."

Trying to allay the difficult news he just disclosed to Mildred, Dr. Jones said, "By the way, Mr. Zuri, here, is a former mountain climbing guide from Africa. How many times did you summit Kilimanjaro?"

Ahgri Zuri suddenly seemed to stand straighter, almost at attention, as Dr. Jones addressed him. With a wide grin, he replied, "I am proud to say that I was on the rooftop of Africa—as Kilimanjaro is known—eighteen times, sir!"

Dr. Jones whistled, and said, "Didn't you work on those coffee plantations as a kid, too? That's supposed to be tough work from what I hear!"

Ahgri Zuri, beaming with delight, replied, "Yes, sir. The sweating, harvesting the beans, cleaning them every day—all day, sunup to sundown—certainly does take its toll on people, especially children. But the coffee bean served me well. It was my pathway to survival and success in my life. So was Kili. Without the difficulties I encountered, I would never have met people like the lovely Miss Dixon, here!"

Dr. Jones smiled, tilted his head to one side, and looked at Mildred, knowing the medical news dampened her spirits. "Miss Dixon, if you have no further questions for now, I will be back to check on you every day and follow the details from the reports I get from Mr. Maizel and Mr. Zuri. They will be my eyes and ears to help you through your stay here."

"One thing, Dr. Jones. When can I go home? I miss my home so much! If I must die now, I don't want to die in a hospital. I want to die at home . . . please!"

Dr. Jones, without uttering a word, came over and gave her a tight hug that lasted for at least a minute. Neither said anything; then Dr. Jones disengaged, looked at her with a benevolent smile, and said, "We will work hard to try to do that. We need to make sure you are stable and strong before we can send you home. Just keep praying and be strong, Miss Dixon. Good night, I'll see you tomorrow."

He opened the door for Annie and left.

Ahgri Zuri and Mildred Dixon looked at each other. Somewhat dejected, she asked the medical student to please finish his life story later. "I need to digest this a bit, if you don't mind," she said.

"Of course! Certainly, Miss Dixon. If you would like to converse, I am a good listener. I do not have answers for the medical issues we are dealing with, but I am most willing to listen."

Mildred's eyes were filled with tears. "Thank you, Ahgri," she said softly. "I really want to hear your story soon. Maybe tomorrow, okay?"

"*Lala Salama*, Miss Dixon."

22

The switchback trail leading up to Kibo's cone—one of three volcano cones atop Kilimanjaro—was narrow, steep, and treacherous: three feet wide in most places and one to two in others.

Almost four hours passed since the seven climbers, three guides, and one porter made their way through the darkness using bright headlamps to illuminate the path directly in front of them. The light revealed deep grooves and ridges with scattered protruding rocks that appeared like little marshmallows bobbing in a cup of hot chocolate.

The grueling, zigzag route that guided them uphill proved to be tremendously taxing on each climber's body, testing their endurance and overall fortitude. They were headed to Gilman's Point, one of three summit destinations on top of Kibo, located at 18,600 feet on the edge of the crater rim. Uhuru Peak, another summit point and the highest position on Kilimanjaro at 19,341 feet, was three and a half miles past the crater ridges.

One of the climbers had incredulously commented at last night's presummit meeting that Gilman was almost a one-mile hike straight up from their Kibo Hut starting point.

"Holy shit! All that in six hours . . . and in complete darkness, wow!" another had replied.

"That's obscene!" most of the climbers said in unison.

Every step forward represented an increase in elevation that created an adverse cumulative effect on the body organs, especially the heart, lungs, and brain called acute mountain sickness. Breathing had become more difficult. The thinning air caused a bit of an ache in the chest and shortness of breath. Many in the group were also suffering from severe headaches as the brain began to swell from the hypoxic environment. All told, excessive fatigue was taking a heavy, detrimental toll on the weary climbers.

Sixteen-year-old Ahgri Zuri was the lead guide on this expedition. Widely known as the Wizard of Kili in local circles and despite his young age, Ahgri had experienced more than most men twice or even three times his age. His demeanor always so calm, voice as soothe as a purring kitten, and his character so reassuring that anyone in his presence would instantly feel calm, comfort, and a sense of warm security. The porters, who assisted his guidance, fondly called him *mama kuku*—mother hen. Much of the credit for these characteristics, Ahgri felt, went to his mixed parentage of a Maasai tribe mother and his Chagga tribe father.

As the group continued to climb in the darkness, he could not help but worry that two of his climbers were not in the tip-top condition needed to successfully complete the summit climb. He kept looking back at his team and frequently reminded them of *pole-pole*. Go slowly!

Last night, during the presummit meeting at Kibo Hut—the base camp for this leg of the climbing route—Ahgri assessed the seven climbers' physical and mental conditions. He took his role as an expedition lead guide seriously and always preached safety first. Adventuresome experiences came in second place and reaching the summit was last on his list of priorities while on the mountain. This was dangerous business, and at any moment, someone could become seriously injured or even much worse. Every year, at least four to seven people died from climbing this mountain—it was surprising that there were no more casualties than that. After all, it was a five-mile hike to get to the top.

Wanting to be a Maasai medicine man since early childhood, Ahgri Zuri took a particularly keen interest in the health and well-being of his climbers. He carefully took care of their wounds and nursed them back to health from their illnesses. He even carefully observed their mental and nutritional well-being. His mother, deceased, would have been so proud of her son.

Abbs, a twenty-three-year-old female climber and medical student from the United States, was one he worried about the most. She was a bit cocky and possessed an aggressive personality, but she had been sick for the past two days with a low-grade fever, a paroxysmal cough, an earache, some vomiting, and now diarrhea, which began that morning. Ahgri was particularly concerned about dehydration and weakness because this portion of the climb required extraordinary strength and stamina because of the rapid vertical gain. The trek to the top was not easy.

"Abbs, would you like to take it easy and stay at the hut while we make the attempt to summit?" Ahgri had asked. "You could just relax and rest. Take in the vista of this mountaintop location. We all know what you have done to get to this point and all of us here admire your incredible courage!"

"Hell no, Ahgri!" she said without hesitation. "I'm not going to stay here!" Her body language was saying, "What's wrong with you? Are you crazy?" "I came halfway around the world to get to the roof of Africa. I'm almost there, and you're asking me a dumb question about staying at this hut while everyone else goes to the top? Are you kidding? And did you forget? I am a fourth-year medical student, so I think I know more about the human body than you do!"

"Abbs, I understand, but you are dehydrated. I am sure you are aware of that condition. I am afraid you will pass out and drag the rest of us down. We would all have to then turn around."

"Well, that's insulting and degrading! I'm going to drag everyone down. Really? I am in the best shape of anyone here, including you, Ahgri. Let me tell you something that'll get you even more nervous about me: I just started my period! That's right, my menstrual period! Yup the menstrual cycle—menstruation—every twenty-eight days! So,

I'm vomiting, having diarrhea, and now having my period. But I'm drinking and eating, so what goes out, I'm putting back in. I will make the climb if I have to crawl. And, if I can't crawl, I expect all of you to drag me up there!" she said. "So, Ahgri, if you want me to stay here at Kibo, you will have to handcuff me to the biggest tree around this ugly hut and tie me up because I'm going up to the top, sir!"

Ahgri looked at her contemplatively, then smiled. "There are no trees up here, Miss Abbs," he said gently.

Everyone laughed at this, effectively breaking the tension between the two and the group.

"So, I guess you will have to go with us, then! Your obvious determination and will power will propel you to the top, I pray!"

"I will go and will beat all of you up that mountain!"

The group cheered and patted them both on the back. Abbs gave Ahgri a hug.

"No hard feelings, right?" Abbs whispered.

"None," replied Ahgri. "Just please do not disappoint me."

His other concern was a man named John Shepard who was in his late sixties. He, too, had an excellent disposition and was a strong-willed man. He had fallen yesterday as they arrived at Kibo. A steady limp was apparent, and Ahgri had to decide about him, too. The injured man, deeply religious, was on this expedition as a fundraising event with his wife to support his church missions.

Ahgri had approached John and talked with him about his concerns. Fatigued and somewhat weary after the five-day hike on the Marangu Route, John said, "Ahgri, I must go. It is God's will that I walk up that hill—it is a hike to heaven and to see God on earth. Many people have donated to our mission, and I don't want to let them down. Please give me a chance to go. I'm aware of the consequences."

His wife, Sarah, stepped in and said, "Ahgri, I will personally escort him back down if this becomes too much for him. I know I can do it. Please give *us* a chance. Please!"

Ahgri told them about AMS—acute mountain sickness—especially the pulmonary edema affecting them, but neither would budge. He finally looked at them both and decided to bring a porter with him in case of an emergency. This way, he could spare one of his guides to escort anyone needing assistance back to Kibo Hut.

The final team consisted of seven climbers, two assistant guides, one porter, and the lead guide as they ascended the steep terrain in the dark of night with an infinite number of stars staring down upon them. The moon was not visible that night.

*   *   *

With another thousand yards to go to reach Gilman's Point, a loud noise disrupted the familiar sounds of the past few hours: heavy breathing, backpacks creaking, and footsteps crunching. Ahgri turned around and, after a quick head count, assessed that one of his climbers was missing. He didn't know who, but called out right away. "John, please answer me, sir."

No one answered.

Abbs said, "He was right behind me just a second ago because I could hear him. I'll go back and find him."

"No! You stay right where you are, Miss Abbs. It is too dangerous; I'm coming toward you and will see."

Just then a moaning voice called out from the dark behind Abbs. It was John. "I'm okay, I just tripped over my own feet just behind Abbs. I think I twisted my ankle! It's very painful! Oh no!"

"Don't move. I will be there right away," said Ahgri. After assessing the injury and a quick overall exam, Ahgri determined that John was a very lucky man and that he suffered a minor sprain of the ankle. It posed a problem, however; he was too high up and too far from Kibo Hut to make it back. Ahgri could not leave him here.

"John, I am going to carry you up to Gilman's Point. Then we will assemble one of our portable stretchers and carry you the rest of the way since it's flatter on the crater rim. So, just stay calm. I have some aspirin in my bag and will give you them now. It will take us another hour to get to Gilman. Your pain should subside a little by then. Stay with me, John Shepard. God is with you, my friend. You are very fortunate you did not roll down this path more. You could have fallen several hundred feet."

"Ahgri," John's wife exclaimed, "how in the world will you carry him? That would be a feat of a superhuman. You are young and strong, but you must be weakened from the climb."

"We have many wise sayings in my tribe such as 'one volunteer is better than ten forced men.' Thus, I am volunteering to carry Mr. Shepard. I am not being forced, so that means I have the strength of ten men who would be forced otherwise. Have faith in me, Mrs. Shepard. I will do this. You shall witness!"

23

The door of patient room 628 suddenly swung open hard, causing it to slam loudly against the interior room wall.

"Okay, Dixon, what kinda night did you have? I don't want to hear a long story, and I really don't care, so don't be long-winded! Tell me how you feel and if anything's bothering you. I'll write it up, then be out of your way for the rest of the day. So, let's get started!"

"Oh my, Sonny Boy! I thought we got past your awful behavior and bad manners! Can you never knock once and give me a proper greeting? Must you always be so boisterous and rude? How do you live a life like that? Just so much into yourself and caring about no one else!"

Jack Maizel had a pounding headache and didn't feel well after a long night of hosting a party with his mother.

"Sorry, you're right! I just had a rough day yesterday and didn't feel much like being cordial."

"You never do," Mildred said curtly. "I cannot imagine how embarrassed your parents must be of you. They must be beside themselves for raising someone so miserable. If I was your mom, I'd be so disappointed that I raised a boy as worthless as gum on a bootheel!"

Jack didn't immediately reply and sat down next to the patient's bed, appearing exasperated, and rubbed his face for a long while. With a deep breath, he said, "Look, Dixon. What you just said about my mother is right on. She says I'm embarrassing to her, and I think I am a disappointment to her. But that's a long story! So, I am sorry. She had a party last night that didn't end well for me, and I got locked up in my room again. I know, I know, you don't know this side of me, but I have constant conflicts with my parents.

"Mom and Dad are the life of any party we ever had. Dad tells people the miracles he performs, and what's worse is they all pay attention and seem amazed and in awe of what he tells them. Of course, they pretend to be in awe of his talents while Mom astounds them with her gaudy collection of expensive antiques and paintings all over the mansion. A jockey rode one of the racehorses into the parlor area and passed out roses to all the women and golden horseshoes to the men.

"Mom and I got into a fight. She was upset that I wasn't talking to anyone. I'm not a good small talker especially with a bunch of people I don't like. They all suck up to me because my folks are rich and influential, and now that I'm going to be a doctor, it elevated my folks another notch in their social world. The funny thing is these people who pretend to like me don't care one bit for me. How laughable is that? I don't like them, and they don't like me, but we all pretend to be interested in what the other person is saying. I think that's called hypocrisy . . . or maybe just plain idiotic!

"I have lived a life of dysfunction, and I just don't know how to get out of it!" Jack paused. "My mother killed my horse, Ajax, when I was twelve years old, Dixon!" Jack suddenly blurted. "She shot Ajax in the head after my beautiful horse broke her leg. It was like my mother couldn't wait to destroy my best friend. It's a long story, so I won't get into it, but it affected me all my life. For the longest time, I wanted to be an animal rights activist and start a sanctuary for animals, but mainly for horses, so they don't have to go to the glue factory when they are old, sick, or hurt.

"Mother was so mad the first time I said that. She told me she didn't want a wandering hippie animal lover as a son and that I better think of a better occupation or I'm going to be homeless. I couldn't even talk to her about it. But I did get counseling and am doing much better these days. Even so, my life is false, lonely, and I'm miserable, Dixon. I just can't take it anymore."

He stared at her momentarily, then said, "Look, I told you I don't like to address you as *Miss* Dixon—I'm gonna still call you Dixon, like I've been calling you. Crucify me if you want, but you'll always be Dixon to me!

"Anyway, I just want out of here. I hate med school. I don't want to be a doctor and don't want to be a horse jockey. Those were the only two choices I could pick from, according to my parents. Of course, the horse jockey reference was a crude joke from my parents. I'm way too big to be a jockey and my folks know it.

"Now, get this, Dixon. They want me to be a doctor, right? But they want me to take over the horse farm when I get older and more established as a physician. So, when I use that argument with them about why would I ever want to be a doctor if I'm going to take over the family farm eventually, they say by then I can just give up my medical life and become a horseman! Is that not nuts, Dixon?

"So, I'm going to go through all this hell just so I can quit being a doctor later and go into the horsing business! That makes no sense to me. Truthfully, I couldn't give a flying rat's ass about that horse farm. I don't like horses anyway. No, I love horses; I mean I don't like racehorses mainly. They are arrogant and prissy. They are treated like royalty; then if they get hurt, they are killed off! It's not that I don't like horses at all. It's that I don't like what happens to them when they get old and slow. They are discarded. Thrown away! My mom likes to use the word *destroyed.*

"If I took ownership of that horse farm, I'd make the entire farm into an animal sanctuary with no more killing of any animals of any kind!"

Mildred Dixon, amazed at Jack divulging so much of his personal information, listened intently and politely to the young man as he poured his heart out. But she reminded herself that what he desperately needed was a sense of purpose in his life. She could see that he was a lost soul. She could also sense a sadness to his being. She wasn't sure what, but he was missing something!

Mildred had to use the bathroom, so she asked that he step out of the room until she finished. When she got back into bed, she called out for Jack to come back into the room. She wanted to change the topic.

"I sense your anger and frustration, Sonny Boy. You know my Bert would have just walked away and left that darn party! If he felt uncomfortable in any way or just simply didn't like the company, he would politely have excused himself and left. Of course, he would always ask me to leave with him since we both shared so much of our thoughts, our likes and dislikes. I would always go along with him. He was a strongminded, strong-willed man and didn't do anything if he thought it went against his core beliefs and his views of purposeful living. That notion of purposeful living was mighty powerful back then, since we never knew when our lives would be taken from us."

Jack softened a bit and relaxed. He seemed interested in Mildred's depiction of Bert. "You've spoken about Bert before. Tell me more. Where did you meet him?"

"His name is Bert Vines, and I met him at Bowman Field in Louisville! Spring of 1942!" she said enthusiastically. "Do you know Bowman, Sonny Boy?"

"Sure, I've heard of it, but never been there. It's a small airport on the south side of Louisville, right?"

She was enthused that she snared Jack's attention. Mildred was now smiling and started to become quite animated while talking and thinking about her past. "Oh, I have to tell you, I wanted Bert badly, Sonny Boy! You know I wasn't a shabby-looking woman myself back then, and I must've caught his eye, too, because he made the first move at a party at the Brown Hotel! That was after my best friend, Helen, tricked him and his friend out of a cab fare. Long story, Sonny Boy.

"The Brown was the place to go and be seen in those days. It was elegant as all get-out! Even after the great flood of 1937 in downtown Louisville, it was just splendid because they restored it to its elegance. Every night they had one big band guest after another while we danced and ate those delicious Hot Browns and cocktails, like sidecars and old-fashioneds, like they were going out of style! Only problem is that we could never hear each other when we just wanted to talk. Sometimes we'd just stroll down to the Ohio River to get some quiet and talk.

"Sometimes when we were wild, we would even go on moonlight cruises on the *Idlewild* steamboat just down Fourth Street off the Brown. It was so romantic, cruising on the river by the moonlight.

"I remember one evening—the most romantic evening of my life— Bert told me a story of a song he heard about the moon. There were a lot of moon songs in those days. It was always romantic. He said that if we were ever apart for a long period, just look at the moon wherever you are, and if we looked at it at the exact same moment, then we were really looking at each other. Oh, how I remember that story and how so romantic that was. I get chills just thinking about it right now. Brings back so many happy memories . . . and so many tears!"

Jack Maizel was mesmerized and was intently listening. He was even grinning. "Wait, Dixon. I've got some questions before you go on. What exactly was Vines's role? What was he being trained for? I think you said he was a bombardier, right? But I'm not sure what that is. And, I think you said 'is' and not 'was' when you described Bert. Does that mean he's still living? If yes, why didn't you guys get together?"

Still sounding peppy, Mildred could not contain her smile and enthusiasm as she dreamily relived her past. She was so happy that Jack was interested enough to ask for more details.

"Great questions, Sonny Boy. You must be tired of listening to an old woman who's living in the past! But I'm glad, and I want to tell you. Yes, we rushed into romance, that was true! Funny, even though we were all in a hurry to find our lifelong mate, we actually liked them and loved them. They were perfect for us!

"Bert often told me, during our intimate times, of his dreams to be an architect after the war. He wanted to build bridges, not destroy them. To him, bridges symbolized hope and connections for mankind. It bothered him to know that he was going to go to Europe to drop bombs on lots of people and, yes, bridges, too. So, he thought that it would be great that someday after the war, he could heal human-ity through building more bridges! Bridges connect people, he would always say.

"War is a curious thing, Sonny Boy. It's about grief, loss, and sadness, but it's also about passion and happiness. Most of all it's about gratitude. Grateful for being alive and being able to love and care about others. That's what life is about! It was so crystal clear for those of us who lived in that period!

"Passion is an important thing in these circumstances, Sonny Boy! Without passion and trust that leads to love, there is no future. That is truly what makes the world go around. It always fuels the flames of purpose."

"So, what happened, Dixon? Why didn't you ever get hitched to this guy?"

Mildred suddenly went a bit sullen. "The war happened, Sonny Boy," she said. "Bert finished his training and left for Europe to drop bombs on our enemies. I was so lonely, and I wanted to be with him so desperately, I decided to apply for the Medical Air Evacuation Transport Squadron and started training in the fall of 1942. I graduated in 1943, hoping to be sent to Europe so I could see my Bert. I longed for him so much.

"Long story, Sonny Boy, but he broke my heart. He broke the engagement and left because he didn't feel worthy of my love. He lost an arm, and he didn't look that great. I didn't care what he looked like. I just wanted to be with him. To start our own family. He said he just wasn't the same man any longer. That he didn't sleep and that he would have these violent episodes. That's when I got interested in battle fatigue and later became a psychiatric nurse.

"I tried to find him; maybe if he could just see me and listen to my plea, he'd change his mind, but I could never find him. He did a good job hiding from me. After a while, I gave up and let him be."

"Well, he's got to be somewhere, right? He couldn't have just disappeared, could he?" asked Jack.

"I think he may have gone back to California, Sonny Boy. I just don't know where he went."

After more conversation, Mildred said, "Sonny Boy. I need to tell you something."

"What is it?"

"I'm scared. I'm scared I won't ever leave here alive. Am I going to die?"

"We don't know what the tests are showing yet," Jack replied. "So, until we do, there's nothing to be scared about."

"Please promise me one thing," Mildred said.

"What's that?"

"If I'm going to die, please find my Bert for me before I go. I want to see him one last time . . . I want to tell him one last time that *I love him* so much . . . and after you find him, please send me home. I don't want to die here. I need to go home to be at my own place. The Chinese have a phrase for having materialistic things aligned just right so that it is in balance with the natural world. Feng shui, they call it. I want to be in my home where there is a feng shui with my spiritual and natural world, Sonny Boy. Please help me find Bert and get me home, please."

24

Mildred Dixon had just finished nursing school at Norton Memorial Infirmary in Louisville and wanted to be a flight nurse but had not been accepted to the program yet. On her first trip to Bowman Field, she was amazed by the vastness of the facility and the amount of airplane and personnel activity.

Her cab pulled up near the administration building of the complex just as there was a sudden cloud burst. She ran to the opening door.

"Hi, Mildred, thanks for meeting me here!" Bert yelled over the rain as he held the door for her. Bert seemed nervous, but he was smiling.

She ran into the building but couldn't avoid being drenched from the rain. Despite a crowd of strangers mingling about, she grabbed Lieutenant Bert Vines with arms widespread. Not uttering a sound, she gave him a wet, passionate kiss, then said, "Happy one-week anniversary, my dear love!"

He continued to keep her in a tight embrace as she relaxed, feeling secure, protected, and loved. She smelled so good, and her lips were so soft. Those pretty eyes caused him to lose his breath while his heart pounded against his chest harder than the rain pelting against the windows. He was beaming with pride, desire, and love for this remarkable woman. As he gave her a bouquet of flowers, he replied, "I love you, my darling. Happy anniversary to you, my dear love."

"I'm soaked and I made you all wet! But you do look handsome when you are wet!" She giggled.

As she attempted to dry off with a handkerchief taken from her purse, Mildred smiled and said, "I haven't been here before. I heard about this interesting building, but I had not seen it yet. What a gorgeous structure this is!" She caught his eyes and lustfully said, "It is almost as gorgeous as you, but not quite, my handsome hunk! I just cannot keep my eyes away from you."

Blushing, Bert Vines said, "This is the administration building of the air facility. I was studying to be an architect in college when I decided to join the army, so I know a little about this design. It's called art deco style and was built in 1929. This movement in architecture first appeared in France around the beginning of this century. The French language and culture is so exquisite, Mildred. This style is called Streamline Moderne because of its curviness and the polished building surfaces. Isn't it a beautiful design—so smooth and clean!

"This building is also the brains of what goes on here with us trainees. My CO has an office upstairs. I'm on the third leg of my training in bombardier school out there." He pointed toward the window and to the airfield where large B-17 bomber planes were parked on the ramp. "And that over there—"

He suddenly stopped. "Oh, how rude of me, Mildred. Come on, I need to get you dried off. I keep talking while you are still soaked from that shower. I'm sorry, my darling. The dining area will have some towels."

As they walked on, Bert seemed excited and nervous at the same time. "Mildred, I found out yesterday that I'm going on to England in the next few weeks to months," he blurted. "There's a bunch of American airbases there. Kind of like their jumping-off place to bomb German territories. They haven't told me exactly where in England, but I suspect it's somewhere in the rural countryside where the US airbases are located. They'll keep it a secret, but know that I'll be somewhere in England.

"They're going to make me a first lieutenant, too. But my point is, I am leaving soon, my Mildred. My bombardier school will be done here soon, and they'll assign me to unit training in England next. Then after that, off to fight the enemy. This means I won't have much more time with you."

They suddenly stopped walking and looked at each other. There was a moment of awkward silence as an avalanche of thoughts went through their heads.

Bert looked down at his feet, shuffling them. He then took a deep breath and peered up at the ceiling. "I don't know how to say this except the only way I know how to say it." He looked at her with deep-set blue eyes in a loving yet pleading manner, a tranquil, soft look that was intensely romantic. "I want to marry you, my Mildred! Please marry me. I need you in my life!" He pulled out a small box from his pants pocket and opened it. There sat a small pear-shaped diamond ring in a holding groove. "I know it's kind of small, but this is just to get us started."

Mildred, stunned by Bert's boldness, didn't know what to say. She was both afraid and excited at the same time. After a quick recovery, she blurted out, "Bert, we just met. I knew that I loved you the very first moment I spied you, but I hadn't thought about marriage."

Bert, now with more composure, said, "There are no rules on how long you need to know a person before they are married, right? You either know or you don't. I knew right away! I fell in love with you the instant I saw you, and I know you did for me, too. I want to spend the rest of my life with you and only you.

"When I first laid eyes on you, I saw your beauty, but I also saw your incredible spirit, kindness, and happiness. I sensed that my life was about to change . . . and all for the good. I could clearly see my future, and it involved us being married, our children playing in the backyard, me working on a new house or building as a much sought-after architect. I see myself designing the grandest homes with unique angles and curves—maybe even some that will look like this building!"

After a moment's pause and looking up as if searching, he said, "And of course bridges. We need more bridges.

"For our own home, I plan to build it on a mountainside where we'll be able to see the earth's curvatures from the top, and we'll grow old there. I want to dedicate my life to you, my darling! So, please say yes!"

Mildred looked at him, with loving tears welling up. "Just one more thing, Lieutenant Vines, before I sign my life to you on the dotted line. There is a war going on. You will be an air warrior, one of the most dangerous of jobs the war can give a man. You are thousands of feet above the ground and dropping explosive bombs on people and places. What if you don't come back? Or, what if something happens to your mind or body, and you just don't love me anymore? What will I do?"

"Mildred, I don't live on suppositions. I live my life from day to day and plan as I always do. If I don't come back, then you will move on and find happiness and peace with someone else. When I do come back, I will sweep you off your feet, and I will love you forever, my darling! I only hope that you feel the same for me and that I will always be in your heart and soul. That is all I ask for, my darling."

She gave him a kiss, looked at him, and said, "Yes, Bert. I will marry you, yes, but I will not marry you until you come back from the war, Lieutenant Delbert Vines. That will give you a reason to come back to me. The French—you say you love the French culture and language, right? Well, they say that each person must have their own raison d'être. Reason for living, Delbert. I want your reason for living to be me . . . to always come back to me. And when you do, I will become your lawfully wedded wife, my dear husband! Yes, we will have children, and I will continue with my career as a nurse, and we will live simply and happily in that mountainside home." She smiled, then gave him a passionate kiss. "Okay, let's see if that ring fits my finger!"

It was a perfect fit.

"Now let's celebrate!" she said. "Take me to the Brown Hotel. I want you to make passionate, fiery, and mad love to me; then after we're done, take me to the bar and we'll sip on an old-fashioned with the best Buffalo Trace bourbon in the house; then we'll share a Hot Brown in the dining room!"

"What in the world is a Hot Brown?" Bert asked.

"Oh, honey, it's the best open-faced sandwich you'll ever have. It was invented at the Brown Hotel! It's made from turkey breast, ham, and bacon, all smothered with creamy Mornay sauce, then baked until the bread is nice and toasty. So delicious, mm-mmm! After that, let's go down to the river and catch a ferry to Fontaine Ferry Park and ride those famous wooden roller coasters."

Bert thought for a second, raised a pointed finger, and said, "Okay, but let's realign the program first. How about if we have the drink and the Hot Brown first, go do the roller coaster ride, then we top it all off at the best room the Brown has and spend a blissful night together?"

"Oh, Bert, that sounds so perfect, but don't you have to be back at base sometime tonight? Won't you get in trouble?"

He smiled a devilish smile, winked his right eye, and said, "I've already taken care of that, Mildred!"

It took her a second to comprehend that he already planned this. "Oh, you're such a mischievous boy, my Delbert!"

He laughed and took her hand as he led her outside into the rain. A bit lighter now.

*   *   *

As the couple snuggled after their romantic and intimate interlude, Mildred whispered, "Delbert, I'm so glad you changed your mind about the order of our agenda! I'm so glad we ate the Hot Brown first, then had those drinks. You know, it made me eager to please you. I didn't really want to go to Fontaine Park anyway. I like this better! It's a better roller coaster ride, and you're not wooden! Eat, drink, make love, talk, then hold each other until we fall asleep!"

Delbert was silent for a few moments, then asked softly, "Mildred, are you okay about what we just did?"

Silence.

After a moment, he said, "I mean, ah, you know . . . having sex before we get married. I'm real sorry for not being more of a gentleman. I should have controlled myself better. I want you to know that I respect you and have the deepest love any man can have for a woman."

Mildred suddenly held him tighter, giving him a physical signal that it was okay. She said, "Hush, my love! I'm sorry that you didn't think you were a gentleman. You not only acted as a gentleman, but you performed like a man! A man who loves his woman deeply with all his heart! I could feel it, Delbert. Not just the physical parts but your emotional being. Your spirit surely entered my soul and transmitted your love to me. For that I am grateful and it makes me the luckiest woman on this planet."

After another tight embrace, Mildred said, "Let's change the subject, Delbert! Let's play *Who are you?*"

"What's that? We didn't have that game in California."

"It's easy, Bert. I'll ask you questions as to what events made you who you are and then you can ask me what made me, me!"

"That sounds made-up, Mildred . . . "

"I go first! So, you told me that you were maybe going to be an architect, but you decided to be a bombardier? How does that happen? Don't bombardiers kill and destroy things from the airplanes? You drop bombs, right? Seems so backward. In one sense you want to save souls and build things of beauty, but what you are doing is destroying things, killing people."

He sighed deeply. "You're right, Mildred. Long story. I was raised in a very Catholic family in Southern California near La Jolla. My ancestors' original name was Vinelli. They were Italians and deeply of the Roman Catholic faith. My grandfather emigrated from Italy and shortened the name to Vines. I was brought up in a Catholic household and was even an altar boy for a long time. I was kind of programmed by my folks to be a priest all through grade school and high school, but one of the nuns who was my math teacher thought I should become an engineer or architect because of my abilities in numbers and my ability to be artsy and creative.

"So, I enrolled in college as an architect major, but one day, we got word that an uncle had been killed by the Japanese. Do you know about the Battle of Wake Island? It was around December 1941, just after the Pearl Harbor attack. We lost that one but not after a valiant struggle by the marines who manned that island and were all heroes. My uncle didn't make it.

"I dropped out of architect school after a year and decided to join the army. I always liked flying and was pretty good with numbers and logic, so I got shuffled into a group that were going to be airmen. Then I was told that since I'm the only one who understood the Norden bomb-sight—a new technology for figuring out precisely where to drop those bombs—they were going to make me a bombardier. I had no idea what that was at the time, but I sure as heck learned about it quickly.

"So that's how I got to be here! How about you, Mildred? Who exactly are you, my love?"

"Just one thing, Bert. An architect is both an artist and a scientist. A person who creates art on scientifically and mathematically structured plans. But you are going to bomb things of beauty—beautiful architecture that's been around for hundreds of years. You are even going to destroy something even more beautiful—human beings. How will you live with yourself, Delbert?"

"I agree, Mildred. I am having a difficult time reconciling this."

Wanting to take the focus away from him, he said, "So enough about me, my love. My turn to hear about you."

"Well, I was born in Corbin, Kentucky, went to first grade there, then moved to just outside of Louisville. I then went to nursing school there. I always wanted to help people, and it gives me such satisfaction. I decided I wanted to help with the war effort, so I volunteered to be a flight triage nurse during the war since they started a program at Bowman Field. One day, I decided to go with my friend to a party at the Brown Hotel, met a beautiful man, and voilà! I am here and going to get married to the most handsome man ever. That's the whole story, Bert. Very boring for someone like you."

"Not at all, my love!" He kissed her, the darkness of the room blanketed their love noises, and the two engaged in intimate passion once more.

25

Precious Jackson, the custodial worker for the internal medicine floor, was busy mopping at the end of the hallway, loudly humming a tune with soothing harmonies, creating a mellow and dreamy effect. The busier she got, the louder the tune became. It was reminiscent of a tranquil Sunday church service as the morning rounding group began to gather. She greeted every person with a huge smile and wished them a blessed day in the middle of her performance.

The rounding group was all smiling and listening when Dr. Jones commanded medical student Jack Maizel to present an update for the next patient.

Charlene, one of the cute, animated young nursing students, asked, "Oh, Dr. Jones, could we just listen to Miss Precious for another moment? I've heard her before—she sometimes starts singing after she hums a bit. She is so good and—"

"No," said Dr. Jones curtly. "Proceed, Mr. Maizel. The lady will stop entertaining once she realizes we are doing serious work!"

Jack glanced at Charlene as she gave him a quick smile and a shrug.

"Miss Dixon, just as a reminder for everyone, is a sixty-three-year-old white female from Corbin, Kentucky, admitted on the first day of September for a spot on her abdominal X-ray. She is here for an evaluation and workup to determine what that spot is," said Jack. "So far, the liver function tests are all elevated, including the bilirubin levels. Her physical exam is consistent with hepatomegaly as evidenced by right costal margin tenderness and liver edge palpable about three centimeters below the margin. Her history is significant for weight loss, abdominal pain that radiates to the back, and jaundice-appearing skin. A GI consult is currently in the works, and we should have a CAT scan result, hopefully by today or tomorrow with the consult report."

Jack Maizel looked at the group expectant of questions, and then Dr. Jones said, "Very good, Mr. Maizel. Very succinct."

Jack smiled. "Thank you!"

"I thought it was really good, Jack!" Charlene said with all smiles.

Dr. Jones smiled, too, but after a few seconds, the smile disappeared. "However." A pause. "Very much backward and much too succinct! The order of information dissemination to your colleagues of physicians or to a group is always history of present illness or HPI, physical exam or PE findings, and laboratory information. You did it completely backward. And to put it mildly, we do not seem to have enough information. I am certain most of us in this circle have similar questions."

Dr. Jones was silent for another moment, then said, "I am curious, Mr. Maizel, as to how you are in your fourth year of medical studies, getting ready to graduate soon, and you are still awkward in your presentation abilities." He looked at him over his glasses. With a faint smile, he said, "Well perhaps, I am a bit presumptuous with that word—*soon.*"

The rounding group snickered and laughed.

"I see that you are not near capable enough to articulate patient information to your colleagues or your attending physician. Why may that be the case, Mr. Maizel?"

Jack Maizel, without missing a beat, replied, "It's called intimidation, Dr. Jones! You intimidate me because of your pompous attitude. You act like you are better than anyone else and know more than all of us collectively. Well, maybe you do, but there are better ways to teach someone how to do something and that would be to show them instead of belittling them every step of the way. You are not so different than my mother. She expects me to be a so-called Burk—a bunch of arrogant assholes who lied, cheated, and stole their way to wealth. They stepped on anyone and everyone who got in their way.

"I have never performed well in situations where I have to be scared into doing a task. How about giving me the benefit of the doubt sometimes? Let me do things, and if I fall on my ass, then I will learn. So, please stop ridiculing me!"

Dr. Jones looked like a cat who had caught and played with his prey, but the catch was fighting back. He smirked. For a moment, Jack imagined he saw a set of sharp horns on Dr. Jones's head, with evil eyes spitting out daggers and bright red saliva dripping down the side of his mouth.

"You must have some other laboratory results back by now, and you must have talked with the GI consulting physicians, correct, Mr. Maizel?" Without waiting for a response, Dr. Jones continued his drilling. "What have you found out? What is your working diagnosis? More importantly, what are your conclusions, Mr. Maizel? I want to know. Please don't keep us in suspense!"

Still fired up, Jack, expecting Dr. Jones's barrage of questions, cleared his throat and clenched his right fist. "Well, Dr. Jones, I think—"

"How is her psychosocial history?" Dr. Jones continued sharply. "Do you know how she's feeling? How is her psychosocial state of being? This is her eighth day here, after all. How is she holding up to all this? Is she asking any questions? Have you related to her at all? How well do you know her as a human being, Mr. Maizel? Have you explored her feelings? Is she depressed about being here, or is she just ecstatic and happy to be around you, Mr. Maizel?"

The rounding team was stunned into silence. No one dared say anything to interrupt the drama between the highly regarded attending physician and the lowly and slovenly medical student.

"Or is she just another patient with a chart number to you, totally devoid of feelings? Please divulge your thoughts. Tell us what you are thinking. I want to know what you want to do with her. Tell us how this will play out, Mr. Maizel."

Jack took a deep breath—feeling, once again, harassed and humiliated by Dr. Jones, just like his mother made him feel. "Look, Dr. Jones, Ms. Dixon is a beautiful human being, and she thinks she's dying. I don't know if she is or not. I happen to think the outcome looks bleak. Nevertheless, I think she should go home. At least get a break from this place. She's been here for a few days now, and she should go home. Why not?"

Surprised and taken aback, Dr. Jones said, "Mr. Maizel, you don't even know what's wrong with her. Certainly, we have verifiable clues and evidence as to what is wrong, but you do not yet have a definitive diagnosis! To send her home now would be a form of malpractice. For example, if she does not have proper support to be resuscitated or stabilized in the event of an emergency, she would easily meet her demise. This situation would not only be medical malpractice but an extreme case of ethical malfeasance. Pray tell, Mr. Maizel. Do you indeed want to send her home? What's wrong with you? You need to know what her problems are first and thoroughly investigate her home support structure before you decide on any discharge planning. You are completely out of your element with her! You are disproportionately out of your mind! Where is your common sense?"

"Look, Dr. Jones, you know good and well what's wrong with Dixon. She's more than likely got some type of cancer with metastatic disease to her liver, and she just wants to go home. More than likely, she will die soon. I just don't want her to die in a strange place with strangers surrounding her. I think she needs to go home to be in the comfort of her house, her surroundings, pictures, smells, friends. . . . Why are we keeping her? What for? There is nothing to do for her right now."

"All you have is speculation at this point. We are all dying to some degree, Mr. Maizel. Our job right now is to get the proper, definitive diagnosis and take the best care we can provide. We can only do this in a controlled environment like this."

"No!" Jack could no longer contain himself. "It's you! You're the one who knows nothing! You're the one who has the heart of an ice cube—for sure a really small one! You're just worried about a frickin' lawsuit! She's not thinking about that. She just wants to go home! Dixon's a sick woman, and we can't do anything for her right now. I say let her go home. And what if she does die? At least it'll be at home, surrounded by her stuff! Bullshit with the law and the administrative policies of the hospital! Let her go home—and if she does die? At least it'll happen in peace! Come on! Dr. Jones, don't be such an ass!"

The other students were stunned and maintained their silence. They turned away. Even Charlene, who had a young girl's crush on Jack, became crimson and looked down at her feet.

"Mr. Maizel, I've had enough of you for now." Dr. Jones's posture became threatening, and his voice grew louder. "This is your last patient for the morning. Please consider yourself relieved and report to my office tomorrow after you get your head on straight! We will go over Miss Dixon's labs and decide how we will move forward with her care. So, we will now disband the morning rounds."

After Dr. Jones stormed away, Charlene approached Jack and said, "Jeez, that was really something. I liked how you stood up for that patient. That took a lot of courage. But I think he is now mad at you, Jack. Do you really think she's going to die soon?" Jack did not respond and after a few seconds, Charlene continued. "You did us proud, though! You kinda let him have it!"

Jack hung his head. Under his breath, he said, "I screwed up again!"

26

Jack Maizel was shocked by what Dr. Jones's said about some of the recent lab reports and findings from the GI consultants. Dr. William Jones had called a meeting with Jack and Ahgri to discuss Mildred's lab and radiological findings.

Jack had thought that his patient only had some mild stomach issues, until some of the preliminary labs started to come in. More recently, it had become obvious that Mildred had something much more serious and that she likely had a cancerous process going on. But now, this was definitive! He was surprised that Dr. Jones had more laboratory and imaging findings than he had known about. Why did he keep them to himself? Jack now had a more complete picture of Mildred Dixon's medical condition after Dr. Jones divulged the rest of the findings. The complete tests, as well as other studies, indicated that she had pancreatic cancer that had likely metastasized to her liver. This was more serious than the colon cancers he had thought about because the death rate was much greater and not much could be done after it had already spread. Jack had so much wanted it to just be a simple stomachache from a virus. *Perhaps the lab results are someone else's,* he thought.

Jack peeked at Ahgri, who sat quietly with his head hanging. He could see tears forming in his eyes.

"I called this meeting with the two of you since you are the primary caretakers for this patient. I know you are the primary acting intern for Ms. Dixon, Mr. Maizel, so I want to hear from you first. What do you think? What is your diagnosis and your differential diagnosis? How do you want to manage this, and what's your prognosis for outcome?"

Jack, still shocked, was speechless and confused. He just couldn't put it all together. A mixture of anger and sadness consumed him, and he felt debilitated. He was angry at Dr. Jones for not being completely open and honest about the other test results and sad for Mildred, knowing her outcome.

"I don't know, Dr. Jones. I mean, what can anyone think? Dixon thought she had something bad like a cancer. I initially thought she could have something tamer like colon cancer. It has a pretty good survival rate if caught early, but I never thought it would be anything terminal like pancreatic cancer! That explains her liver enzymes being up. She has metastasis to her liver, which virtually spells doom for her.

"I do know that she wants to go home and die if she has something bad. She desperately did not want to die in a hospital. I don't know. I just don't even know how to think about this, Dr. Jones. I just checked for those radiology results early this morning, but all I got was the 'pending' remark! I didn't know that you already got them. The results, I mean!"

"Right! Being an attending physician has its privileges, Mr. Maizel! I actually got a call from Dr. Alberti, the senior radiologist, late yesterday. So, to be fair, I did have a heads-up on you. But that's beside the point, Mr. Maizel. You've had lots of time with this patient. You did a complete physical exam and got a good history, and you've been seeing her every day. You must have some insight into her condition."

Squirming a bit, Jack said, "Honestly, Dr. Jones, I remotely thought she could have something bad like pancreatic cancer, but not in my wildest dreams did I believe that's what it was. I think it was wishful thinking on my part. But if it was something this bad, I thought it would be reasonable if she went home, especially if it was terminal. I really thought it might have been a bad case of peptic ulcer or even an irritable bowel syndrome type of thing."

"The lesson here, Mr. Maizel, is you must always approach all ailments and complaints seriously, and you must have a differential diagnosis. There are so many things that can mimic each other. Did you even have a differential on her condition?" Without giving him time to respond, Dr. Jones looked toward the other acting intern. "What about you, Mr. Zuri? Any clues? What do you think about Miss Dixon?"

Ahgri Zuri tilted his head back upright and wiped tears from his eyes with the back of his hands. He said, "Miss Mildred's condition warrants a differential diagnosis of, yes, IBS—irritable bowel syndrome, for sure, as Jack indicated, or even peptic ulcer disease. I felt that colon or stomach cancer was far-fetched. I never thought about pancreatic cancer, either. In retrospect, other conditions that should have been considered upon admission include some form of neoplastic activity, such as pancreatic cancer, hepatitis, perhaps a hepatoma, bowel cancer. In this case, after your disclosure of the radiological findings, she obviously has a form of cancer. Pancreatic—and fairly advanced, I fear. It is my understanding that because we have difficulties with early diagnosis of this disease, it is usually in an advanced form once we detect it."

He stopped for a second for effect. "As far as her management, I think it would be most humane if we let her die and not go through the usual rigors of chemotherapy, radiation therapy, and surgery. Her prognosis is already very poor."

He stammered for a moment, then added, "She, more than likely, will die from this. I would let her go home and die in peace, too."

"Very perceptive and excellent presentation, Mr. Zuri! But we are doctors, and we must do everything we can to help this poor soul. For both legal and ethical reasons, we would not send her home. If we send her home now, we certainly will open ourselves for litigation. The opposing legal team will make the argument that we sent someone home from the hospital without treating or attempting to treat.

"The current convention is to get her on chemo and possibly radiation. Surgery is probably not an option. As you said, it is fairly advanced and metastasized into surrounding organs, including the liver. So, we will need hematology oncology specialists and the radiation medicine folks consulted and see what they think. We are a hospital and have a moral, legal, and ethical obligation to support life until it ends."

Dr. Jones then turned back to Jack. "So why are you so confused, Mr. Maizel? It is quite obvious what's going on, as Mr. Zuri described. I do want to know what you are thinking. Please remember that you are training to be a doctor, Mr. Maizel, and you must maintain composure and a clear level of thinking abilities in front of the patients. I don't want an emotional outburst from you as was on display in yesterday's rounds.

"You know, I should suspend you for your outburst yesterday, but after thinking about it last night, I am proud of you for standing up for your patient. I'll let it go for now!"

Jack's face heated, and he suddenly stood up. "Bullshit! Don't do me any favors, Dr. Jones! This is nothing but bullshit! Look, I never asked for this, and I never wanted to be a doctor! My parents told me I had to be one, and I'll tell you, I hate every minute of the damned profession!

"Sure, I'm not the dumbest guy to put on one of these clown-like clinical jackets. I can figure out that what we are talking about is bad stuff—duh! Dixon is a very sick woman, and with my limited knowledge of medicine, I don't think we can do anything for her! She's a dead woman! And, yeah, even though I'm wearing this stupid white coat and got some science knowledge about people, I got emotions and feelings, too.

"I feel bad. Real bad, and I should be able to show it if I want to! It shouldn't matter what I am! It shouldn't matter that I'm in the medical profession or if I'm on some road construction team; I feel bad for this lady! And, listen, I'm no fricking shrink kinda doc, but I think they'd say it's supposed to be healthy to express your emotions! So, bullshit about conventions! She's a sick woman; she's dying and—what, we're going to pretend like we're helping her by being some sort of cardboard-cutout doctors and give her some drugs that we can't even pronounce the name of? We all know that it won't do anything except that it'll make her sicker and the rich drug-peddling folks richer!

"What about her quality of life, Dr. Jones? So, we don't care about that? She needs to go home to be around her stuff, her smells, her pictures, and her family! She doesn't want to die in an institution in a strange bed with strange curtains. She doesn't want to die with strange smells and strange noises everywhere around her. And she certainly doesn't want all these strange people who roam the halls of hospitals like you, Dr. Jones, around her!

"She just wants to go home! She wants to die at home! For God's sake have some decency and let her do that! *Please!* One more thing, Jones! Okay, Dr. Jones . . . years ago, I turned my back on my best friend and let her die. I let my mother destroy her. I'll be damned if I let this happen again without my going to bat for Ms. Dixon. Send her home!"

He was angry and had to pause for a second. "Is this what the profession of medicine is all about? Can it be so cold and hardcore? Why don't we take any consideration for emotions or feelings? So, that's what I think, *Dr.* Jones! And you know something else, this is what I think about this hospital and your conventions. It's such bullshit!" Jack raised his middle finger toward Dr. Jones. "You don't know jack shit about humanity! You're like a robot and only understand black-and-white stuff only!"

Dr. Jones sat there, staring at Jack, and listening to his outburst. He showed no emotions. Then, a grin gradually came over his face. "Unfortunately, you are correct, Mr. Maizel. There is very little room in the science of medicine to waver. We must follow strict protocols. If we don't, we can be construed as providing malpractice. This is the danger of wavering and giving into our emotions. However, I want to tell you, well said, Jack."

He then got up, dismissed the two acting intern medical students, and walked out of his office.

As the two students exited Dr. Jones's office, Ahgri, befuddled, looked at Jack and said, "*Adui aangukapo mnyanyue.* When your enemy falls, lift them up. He has fallen to your thoughts, Jack, because you are right. He knows as well as we do that Ms. Dixon should go home, but he is too ingrained in his processes of how medicine works. He may be hampered by some medical-legal issues, but overall, he is a self-imposed prisoner of rules, duty, and convention of the medical world. So, now, let's listen to his wisdom about medicine and thank him by lifting him up above us. I think he is a good man, and I am proud of you both."

Jack nodded and shrugged. He mumbled, "Whatever."

When they got to the other end of the hallway, Ahgri said, "I thought you were a crazy man, Jack, when you confronted Dr. Jones. I was certain you would get dismissed from the program! But fortunately for you, I think he appreciated your comments. I do have one question, Jack. Why can you just not let things go? Why must you react to everything and then get in trouble for your behavior? You are, as they say in this country, a hot head! In my country, you are a *pumbaa* . . . a very large *pumbaa* with no hope . . . ever!"

"I've been a loner since I lost my best friend as a child. It hurt so bad when they came to kill her after she broke her leg in a riding accident. She was on top of the world, Ahgri! She won that dressage event, but Mom just . . . poof . . . extinguished my Ajax! The sad thing is she died alone—without me! Without the one person who loved her! Poor Ajax had no one around to say goodbye. If Dixon has to die, she needs to let it happen somewhere she loves, somewhere that is near and dear to her heart. I don't want her to die alone, Ahgri! I will do my best to be with her when that happens!

"You know, after Ajax was killed, I was in a bad way and went to counseling for years. They said I was traumatized and was never the same kid after that!"

"Yes, I recall that story and how traumatic that was for you."

"Ajax was my best friend and an all-around great horse! Anyway, after I got better, I decided that I would always be the champion for wayward animals and people. So, I will not let Dixon down! She wants to see Bert, and she wants to go home, and I will find him and get her home! I won't let her die alone!"

Neither man said anything for a few minutes, letting their thoughts and emotions simmer down. Finally, Jack Maizel said, "She does grow on you, doesn't she, Zuri? I don't want to see her getting sick over these chemo drugs. It won't do her any good, right?"

Ahgri replied, "No, they won't, Jack!"

27

"Come in, Sonny Boy!"

The door opened gently, and Jack walked in.

"How d'ya know it was me, Dixon?"

"I could sense that it was you when I heard footsteps outside of my room. Anyway, they're your footsteps! Did you know that everyone has their own signature footsteps? It's a lot like fingerprints—we all have peculiar ways of walking. It has to do with style and flare! Besides, no one else visits me except you and Ahgri. . . . He's so quiet—out of respect for others—you'd never know that he was in the room. That's why I have a great chance to get it right, right? Okay, now tell me, what can I do you for?"

"That's an odd way to ask a question, Dixon—'What can I do you for?' Sounds a bit colloquial, like the old Western TV shows."

"That's funny because I was watching some Westerns on the television set, and those cowboys always said things like that. I kinda like it!"

As Jack sat, he asked, "You know, after we had that long conversation the other day, I was wondering, why don't you have any family? Why don't you ever get visitors?"

"Everyone died, and I never got married. I told you that already. Bert kinda left me, so I don't have kids is the simple answer."

"I know that from your admission records and intake history. I guess I just want to know if you've got a family. You know, like brothers, sisters, nieces, nephews . . . anyone? And how come you don't have a hubby, Dixon? Wasn't there ever anyone else after your fling with Bert? No one else wanted you? Are you that difficult to get along with?" joked Jack.

"You're so funny, ha!" Mildred mocked the laughter.

She looked up for a moment, as if she were reminiscing, and then looked at Jack. "As I already told you, much of the passion that Bert and I had was due to the newness of a relationship and the urgency and unknown about what would happen to us because of the horrifying war. That became the forefront of our lives. After Bert didn't want to see me any longer, I never had the desire or passion to fall for another fella. It took the wind right out of me! I never wanted anyone else!

"Speaking of passion—seems like we've been talking a lot about it, but it is so important for our lives. I've been wanting to tell you a fun story about passion that led to a significant purpose in a man's life that I once had the immense privilege to know. I think it may help get your life's *compass* together, Sonny Boy."

Mildred rolled her eyes upward as if recollecting her thoughts, then said, "His name was Willie Smallwood. An extraordinary man driven by passion and purpose. A strong belief in himself.

"When I was a little girl in elementary school, we were required to go to moral training on Wednesdays. Well, maybe we weren't required, but most kids went. We had to line up according to the religious denominations our parents wrote on the permission slip. I was in the Baptist group but wanted to be in the Methodist gang because they were way cooler and more fun.

"We'd all get in our lines, and head out on foot to our churches. All the kids went, save a few here and there. There were always a couple of Jewish kids. We didn't seem to have any Muslims, Buddhists, or atheists in those days, especially in rural Kentucky.

"Once we got outside, there was always a young man hanging around—maybe in his mid-twenties—who we'd call Willie. His legs were really skinny and didn't work right, so he sat and rolled around on a board with wheels that looked like one of those creepers that go under a vehicle when you work on them.

"We nicknamed him Creepy Willie. It fit him pretty well because he was kinda creepy, rolling around on the board and following us everywhere we went. He was actually very friendly, but some of us were still scared of him. His unshaven and dirty face gave him a sinister sort of look. Some of the adults including our teachers even said his mind was slow and that we shouldn't be around him.

"Creepy Willie had a habit of doing a real unusual thing—at least that's what we thought at the time. He picked up trash, up and down the roadways, in people's yards, in the ditches—almost everywhere he could get to. He told everyone he loved to pick up trash to make everything sparkling clean for us and the animals. He did this day and night—every day and every night. No wonder the adults thought he was a little bit of a nut. The nicer word to describe him is *eccentric*.

"A few years later, the town honored him by giving him an award—Mr. Clean of the Year Award! They gave him a hundred-dollar check, a nice write-up in the local papers, and a very nice plaque declaring that he was an outstanding citizen. What people didn't know was that he would also find Coke bottles along the roadways, and he'd turn them in for bottle refunds. It was usually a penny or two per bottle back then. But if you found a lot of them, it built up and things didn't cost as much back then. Willie was an economic and business whiz! Over a lot of years, he made a hefty amount of money. It goes back to that saying about how someone else's trash is someone's treasure! Willie Smallwood had a great understanding that garbage can be turned into cash!

"Between what he earned and those who just gave him money because of his notoriety, plus the people who just plain felt sorry for him because of his legs, Willie eventually got some help for them. They put braces on him, and he had a few surgeries. After that, he started to get around a little and then got a job with the local garbage service. He told everyone that he worked as an engineer. When they pressed him about what type of engineer he was, he laughed so hard, then told them that he was a sanitary engineer, otherwise known as a garbage collector!

"Well, wouldn't you know it, he became very successful and started his own garbage service and put the others out of business. He became rich and eventually ran for and won the mayor's race for our town! Yup, Mayor William Smallwood! He changed his name from Willie to William, believing the name should fit with the status. 'Nicest man you'll ever meet!' was his motto.

"I tell you this story, Sonny Boy, because this man was nothing. A nobody. No education, no money, no family, nothing! But he had passion and purpose. He loved picking up garbage. He was fascinated by it! Loved it so much that he ended up making a career over it and then became very successful. That's what passion is about, and that's how it helps you succeed. It's fuel for life, and it is darn flammable! Just ignite it, and you will explode into success and happiness. You will have the world, Sonny Boy. There will be no stopping you, sir!"

The medical student just shook his head and said, "Wow!"

"Let me ask you something, Sonny Boy. Do you know the difference between an alligator and a crocodile?"

"Are you kidding?" asked Jack. "They look exactly alike to me. And, besides, I couldn't care less. Why do you even ask me that, Dixon?"

"Just as I suspected! Didn't you specialize or major in some kind of science in your undergraduate studies?"

"Well, yeah, I was a biology major because it was a breeze and pretty easy!"

"But you didn't care anything about it, did you? You weren't passionate about it, right? You took it because it came easy to you, and it was a stepping stone to medical school—something your parents wanted you to do?"

"Okay, you got me, Dixon. I know what you're gonna say and where you're going with this. Because I wasn't passionate about biology and I really didn't care to know the difference between those two ugly creatures, it makes me a bad biologist."

"That's right! My point is, you cannot do anything well if you don't have passion and purpose. That's one of those laws of nature, Sonny

Boy! Learn it and embrace it, and you will be happy and go far! Right now, you're missing that in your life. Passion will lead you to purpose every time, and the heart will tell you what to do. Always go with your heart and not with your brain. The heart is the brain when it comes to passion and the spokesperson for your soul. It will never, ever steer you wrong. Remember that, Sonny Boy. Just follow that simple plan. You will be a good doctor if you follow that path.

"So, let's get to the bottom of this topic—have you ever thought what your purpose in life is? Is it that you really want to be a doctor to help humanity, those that are suffering? Do you really have a passion for medical science and making the downtrodden better? You need to think about that, Sonny Boy. Your heart will tell you! You won't ever be happy or fulfilled without feeling for something!" Mildred paused for a moment, looking contemplative. "It seems to me that your passion was your horse, Ajax. I'm not telling you to be a horse person, but that is your passion and purpose. I think you need to think long and hard about what you want out of life, Sonny Boy.

"You just won't and can't do a good job at anything if you don't have a thirst, a hunger for what you are doing. This brings me back to my Bert and why I decided to stay unmarried." She touched and toyed with the ring dangling from her necklace. "I loved this man with all my heart and soul. We did not marry in a civil court or church, but we spiritually married, and as far as I'm concerned, I belong to Bert. He is the love of my life. There is no other man for me, Sonny Boy.

"Please promise me one thing, Sonny Boy. If this whole business of me being here doesn't go well, please know that there is only one thing I want. I want to see Bert just one more time so I can tell him that I love him. But there is one thing I do not want: I don't want to die here. I just want to be left alone at home. Please help me with that, Dr. Jack Maizel."

Jack sat quietly, took everything in, and tried to formulate a response, but nothing came. *She is right! What am I doing? Why am I in medical school? Do I really have a passion for it? Mildred knows what she wants. She even knows what she doesn't want. What a remarkable woman!*

Just then, Jack's pager went off, directing him to call an extension number.

"Okay, I need to go, Dixon, but I came here to tell you something important before I leave. This is a hard thing for me to talk about since I don't have any experience in these sorts of things, but I got some bad news."

"Oh? What is it?" asked Mildred Dixon.

"We got some test results back and had a team meeting with Dr. Jones, our attending physician. It shows that you got cancer. More specifically, it's pancreatic cancer, Dixon. The problem is, we don't know how long you've had it and if it's even spread."

The medical student did not disclose the rest of the information about the spread of the disease. He felt another time would be better. It was too emotional for them both to go into it now.

Mildred's face did not change—showing no emotions. She just looked at the medical student. In a flat affect, she replied, "Well, it is what it is, Sonny Boy. Now you need to go, but I'm going to have some questions later, I'm sure. I need to let the news sink in."

"I'll be back soon, Dixon." He touched her hands, attempting some comfort, then left, exhaling deeply.

28

The weather turned cooler over the past week as temperatures fell to a low of 37 degrees. The airport wind sock, blowing toward the southeast, was lit up by a three-quarter moon surrounded by a star-filled sky. Buildings and airplanes were silhouetted by the darkness combined with the moon and stars' luminescence, giving them an eerie glow. Even the fine curves of the administration building had an eerie look in the moonglow.

Lieutenant Van Miller and Mildred Dixon were shivering as they walked briskly across the tarmac toward the edge of a runway where the mammoth B-17 bomber was parked. He nervously looked around and urged Mildred to walk faster. "If they catch us, we're in big trouble!"

The fast pace, almost a trot, winded Mildred, but she did her best to keep up. "Thank you for setting this up for us, Van! You've become a real sweetheart! I'm so glad we became friends after all. You were such a jerk in that cab that day we all met, but you turned out A-okay!"

"Yeah, Bert owes me plenty, believe you me, Mildred! And you . . . you turned out to be a great gal—not like that Helen friend of yours!" he replied with a frown. They both laughed.

"You know, when we got our orders late last night informing us that we pull out at oh-six-hundred for England, Bert blurted out that he had to see you once more before he left the States. He was almost in tears. I felt awful for him, so I said I'd take care of it, and that I'd make arrangements for you two to meet on the bomber by oh-four-hundred!

"I nearly jumped out of my pants when I found out you were on base as part of that flight nurse training program. After that it was easy to get a hold of you and put everything in motion. We still got to be careful since we're not authorized to be out right now. You know, it's a curfew kind of thing."

After a few more minutes, they came to the airplane's entry door located toward the rear of the airplane, just in front of the horizontal stabilizers. Van banged on the door three times and opened it as Bert appeared inside the cabin.

"Van, I cannot thank you enough." They shook hands; then Bert grabbed Mildred with a big hug. "I missed you so, my dear Mildred. Welcome to my abode." He waved his arms toward the front of the cabin. "Let me show you around my palace, dear queen." They both laughed.

Van said, "Okay, you're on your way, honey! You two have an hour. That's sixty minutes starting now; then you'll hear three bangs under the front hatch at the bottom of the fuselage just below the pilot's compartment. Bert will help you get through that hatch, and I'll be waiting for you here on the ground. Sorry, but we got to do it that way because we're leaving at the butt crack of dawn and the rest of the crew will be coming for takeoff prep. It's kinda funny that everything seems to always happen under the cover of darkness. That's when all the good stuff happens anyway, right?" Van said, chuckling. "If we are all clear, I'm skedaddling. You kids have fun!"

The couple nodded, and Bert shut the door.

*   *   *

Forty-five minutes rushed in the blink of an eye. They made eager love—clawing, kissing, touching, and hugging. They desperately clutched on to their mate's body, tightly bound their arms and legs around each other, knowing soon they would have to let go. They panted. Each screamed and both cried on their way to a splendid climax followed by the pleasing release of tension and calmness. It was as if an ocean storm had violently swept over, soon followed by languid ocean waves stroking the beach ever so softly.

As they lay on a makeshift blanket that covered a small section of the plane's fuselage floor, Bert whispered, "My dear Mildred, I will miss you, but I'm comforted by my deep love for you. It is forever sealed in my heart and soul."

"Delbert, I want to give you this two-dollar bill. I heard a romantic story once about a man who gave his wife a two-dollar bill before he left for war. He tore the top corner off and kept that piece but gave the bill to his wife, saying that when they got back together, they would make it whole again.

"I want to do that, too. So, I want to give this to you, and I am going to tear the corner and keep it. You hold on to the two-dollar bill, and when we are back together once you get home, we'll use tape to put it back together and then celebrate at the malt shop ice cream parlor and listen to our favorite songs on the jukebox!"

Bert kissed her, took the bill, folded it twice, and put it in his wallet. "It will always be with me until we meet again.

"I want to give this to you, my love." He reached into a jacket pocket. "Not long after I met you, I realized you were my one and only and forever. I started making this ring for you. It's a '42 Jefferson nickel. It took me until about a week ago to finish it. I was hoping that I could give it to you before I left. It is my wedding band to you. It has silver in it, so it may tarnish a bit. I want you to wear it. I want this to be your wedding band."

"Delbert, this is beautiful." She started sobbing. "How in the world did you make this? Out of a coin? It's beautiful. You can see the year and the words 'In God We Trust.'"

"Good eye, Mildred." He held her hand tightly. "I wanted to keep the 1942 to signify when we met, and in front of God, who we trust, will we declare our love for each other and be united in marriage forever."

"Delbert, I don't want to put this on my finger until you come back and marry me. I want you to put that ring on my finger then. For now, I will wear it as a necklace. Could you make another one, Delbert, for yourself so I can put it on your finger when we say our wedding vows?"

He yanked something out of his pocket and said, "Look, I've already started, and it'll be finished when I get back to you." He then pulled her toward him, and they hugged deeply.

Thump, thump, thump!

The noise startled them. Their time was up. Both shed tears unashamedly.

"Please take care of yourself. Be safe, my Delbert. I want you back in my arms, my precious darling! I want you to come back to me soon and stay forever. Godspeed to you, my love!"

29

Jack Maizel knocked softly and entered room 628.

"I came back, Dixon," he declared.

Mildred was lying on her back, staring at the ceiling as if in a trance. She had been crying—that was obvious to Jack.

Without looking at Jack, she said, "It's a sort of sandwich! Kind of an open-face type. It has turkey, bacon, and Mornay sauce. Some people like to substitute ham or just add to it. A lot of people like cheese sauces instead and maybe even add a slice of tomato to it. It's *so* good, Sonny Boy!"

Confused, Jack said, "What are you talking about, Dixon?"

"The Hot Browns I told you about. The best sandwich in the world! It was invented by a fella named Fred Schmidt in 1926. He made it exclusively for the Brown Hotel, but everyone who grew up in Louisville knew about it. It was famous! Many nights, after we danced, kissed, even made out a bit, we had a few cocktail drinks of sidecars—made with the best Cognac ever. I think Hennesey makes the best ones.

"But anyway, those Hot Browns filled our appetites and having alcohol sitting in our bellies made us all a bit happy and probably a little crazy! Bert could somehow always eat two of them! Goodness, I don't know how that fella could eat all that!"

She laughed and then sighed. A momentary awkward silence filled the air. Both felt it, but neither breached the subject of cancer.

"Thanks for coming back so soon, Sonny Boy!" She sighed deeply. "Let's get rid of the pink elephant in the room, shall we?"

Jack, with half a grin, said, "I thought it was the eight-hundred-pound gorilla in the room?"

"Sonny Boy! I declare, you're not too up-to-date on your animal idioms! The gorilla reference has to do with something so big—like a government or maybe a business that can't be removed or put in its place because it's so big. Thus, the intruder does not budge, and nothing gets done. The pink elephant in the room has more to do with an awkward situation that everyone is aware of but no one wants to talk about it. So, this one has to do with the pink elephant called cancer!

"I'll get right to the point. Your boss, Dr. Jones, came by not long after you left. He was straighter with me than you were, and he cut right to the chase. I suppose I prompted him to be that way because I looked straight in his eyes and told him to not dare lie to me."

Just then, as if on cue, Dr. Jones walked in after a knock.

"Speak of the devil!" she said. "So now I have you both in the same room. Let's get this out in the open, and I want you both to be honest with me. First, I want to thank you, Sonny Boy, for being forthright and explaining the dreaded cancer I have, but you didn't tell me the full extent of it. Yes, I know, you probably felt bad and awkward to even tell me. I understand. But later, Dr. Jones, here, comes in and, as a more direct man, tells me that I cannot beat this cancer because it's spread to my liver and probably other places. He pointed out that I have a bad prognosis since we're getting to it so late in the game. That's why my skin's so yellow and my belly aches so!

"I told him that I know what metastatic cancer is and that he doesn't have to explain it in more detail! I got angry with him and kicked him out." She turned to him and said, "Sorry, Dr. Jones. I'm glad you humored me by coming back to see me. I'm just in a bad way with my mood right now."

Dr. Jones nodded and said, "No harm done, Miss Dixon."

"So, now since I have you both here, I want to know your opinions. Dr. Jones, I know you are the boss, but you don't strike me as a warm and fuzzy man. Sonny Boy, you are not too experienced and so very young, but sometimes innocence is pure. Your decisions and conclusions come from the heart while age brings wisdom of experience, but sometimes, we have too much information and knowledge. I believe that they may cloud our decision. You know, too much clutter in our minds.

"I think you have a lot of passion about things, Sonny Boy. That's why you get in trouble so much. So please tell me what you think I should do. You go first, Dr. Jones!"

"Thank you, Miss Dixon. I do not appreciate being put on some sort of trial, but I am curious about where exactly you are going with this since I am the one who makes the decisions here and neither one of you can trump me. This is how we will proceed. We will need to get our surgeons to do a laparoscopy to see how widespread your cancer has gone. We then bring in our oncologists and start the first rounds of chemotherapy followed by radiation. As we get the spread controlled, we can then be more specific with the overall management."

"Thank you, Dr. Jones. Sounds like you are reciting from a medical textbook!" Mildred replied with a bit of sarcasm. "From a patient's perspective, that is *not* how I want to spend my last days on earth. You make me feel like a laboratory animal that you want to experiment your drugs on just to see how long you can keep me alive! That's after you already told me my outlook is poor. You may get your kicks that way, sir, but I am the one who suffers while I die."

Dr. Jones looked uncomfortable and he avoided eye contact with Mildred.

"Okay, how about you, Sonny Boy? What say you?"

He looked contemplative for a moment, then replied, "I want to apologize to you, Dixon. I didn't want to disclose everything because I wanted to have a talk with Dr. Jones about my way of thinking about your condition. He and I had a disagreement about your care. I know he is the seasoned and smart doctor, but in my opinion, he's a brutal man when it comes to being nice to patients and being empathetic. Dr. Jones is rude and tactless, in my opinion. Look, he just told you that you have no say-so about your care. Come on, he's the boss, of course, and he does have the controls! But it is your body and your life. No one can tell you what to do, Dixon!"

Dr. Jones threw eye daggers at Jack and said, "You are dismissed, Mr. Maizel. Take leave from this patient's room! Now!"

"Not so fast, Dr. Jones. I am the real boss here as Sonny Boy explained. Not you. It's my body and not yours." Mildred looked at them both and laughed. "This is so much like the counseling sessions I used to hold with my patients. Funny, an old patient counseling two medical people! This is getting fun! So, you are saying that Dr. Jones doesn't have bedside manners, but you do, Sonny Boy? And you are tactful? Please don't make me laugh any more. My belly hurts too much for that!"

"I meant from a sympathetic point of view," Jack retorted. "For example, I didn't tell you about the spread because I thought it would be better if I gave you one piece of news at a time. Plus, like I said, I wanted to see if I could get Dr. Jones to support me with what I had in mind for you. You know that is to let you absorb small bits of information instead of all the bad news at once! And, finally, I want to get you home to where you want to be. I just thought that would be more humane.

"Dr. Jones wants to do things that's in textbooks. I want to take care of you to give you comfort and peace. He will be aggressive with your care and do all the bells and whistles including chemo, radiation, and maybe even some surgery as he mentioned. I say, the cancer has spread too much and all that work on you may prolong your life for a few days. But what's the quality of life? I can tell you: I've seen people on chemo, and they are sicker than a stray dog! They're puking and miserable. I don't want you to be miserable, Dixon!"

She looked at him with sad but loving eyes. "Sonny Boy. I feel the exact same way. I just want to go home now. But there is one thing I want more than anything before I go home."

She didn't say anything for a few moments. Dr. Jones nodded to both Jack and Mildred and said, "I need to leave. You are both correct, and I stand corrected. I will leave you both to yourselves." He then quickly made his exit.

"I do know what you want," Jack declared. "You told me already. You want to see Bert."

"Yes, I want to see my dear Bert once more before I die. I love him so much, and I don't want to leave this earth without seeing him just one more time. Would you find him for me? *Please*, Jack. Please!"

Jack, now fighting back tears, replied, "Yeah. Sure, Dixon, I'll find him for you."

He couldn't help but think how he left Ajax with his mom and let her kill his beloved friend. He didn't even try to fight off the two men who carried him away. *I abandoned her, and I won't let it happen again!* He let them drag him away—like a helpless child. Not this time. He was going to do everything in his power to deliver his promise. This was his passion and purpose!

"Thank you, Jack! My dear Sonny Boy! I am going to sleep now. Tomorrow is a new day, and I will have something to look forward to. I will reset myself and will look forward to seeing him one last time!

"Good night, my dear Sonny Boy. Happy dreams to you."

I'll make this happen! thought Jack.

30

The man strolled across the cafeteria entrance with head held high, just like a fierce Maasai warrior would . . . and should. Tradition and memories were important to honor and respect his past and carve out his future. Ahgri Zuri was a proud man.

While the noise and the clutter of daytime activities began to fade, the dimly lit cafeteria was a welcome respite for any busy hospital worker. It had the air of a lazy evening, a place where a person could retire for the day and lounge around on a big soft couch while watching late-night reruns until they fell asleep.

Ahgri grabbed a cup of coffee from the vending machine, took a sip, and frowned. He made his way to where Jack Maizel sat. "You know, Jack, this coffee is simply atrocious! The best coffee in the world is grown in Tanzania on the lower slopes around Mount Kilimanjaro. It is the perfect altitude for the coffee bean plant to grow. Many years ago, Germans came to my country and established many coffee plantations. They hired our people to work on these estates. The work was hard, but they were very good to my people.

"We love arabica coffee. It goes down smoothly and warms the soul! It is the best! I can still smell and taste its goodness! This coffee I am drinking from a machine that does not bother to acknowledge me or offer a thank you is nothing but a freeze-dried version of synthetic coffee. It is not even real!"

He closed his eyes and drew a deep breath, smiled, and shook his head slightly. Then, opening his eyes, Ahgri smiled broadly. "The machine does not even smile!" He laughed.

After he settled in a chair directly across from Jack, he asked, "Why are you sitting here by yourself in the semidarkness, Jack? What are you doing here? You are not on call tonight; should you not be home in bed by now?"

"I was waiting to catch up with you, Ahgri. I need to discuss something with you. You're my only friend—my only true friend, that is, and I trust you completely to be honest with me. You are such a wise person. I think you got that way from all your tough childhood, right? You don't ever mince words, and you're always brutally straight with me—even if it's bad stuff, right?

"So, I start by telling you that I'm a little down, kind of depressed, you know. I need a good talk with you tonight. I need and want you to be straightforward with me and tell me what I am doing wrong with my life. You game for that?"

"Certainly, Jack. You are my friend, so I want you to tell me what's on your mind. Is it about Miss Mildred? She has gotten underneath your skin, has she not?"

"Yes. There is something about that lady. She has a way of striking certain punches at my emotional nerve centers. It's as if she knows how to bring out my feelings—good, bad, and sad ones. She's had a rough life and a lonely one, too. She had a love interest at one time—they were engaged but didn't marry because he went to war. He came back but was apparently quite disfigured, and he didn't think he was worthy enough to marry her. Dixon wants to see him one last time before she dies. I think I can help her get her death wish. Wouldn't it be nice if I could find Bert for her?

"We also had a long conversation about passions and purpose. She called me a loser and accused me of not having any goals in my life. She said I'm a guy without passion and that I have no feelings.

"I wasn't sure what she was talking about at first. I never thought of myself as some kind of loser, but she's right. I'm just not my own person—my own man! Hell, Ahgri, what am I doing in med school, anyway? I hate it. I hate it with a passion . . . so, she's wrong in that way. I've got passion. Maybe it's the wrong kind! But my passion is to hate things. I hate medicine, I hate Jones, and I even hate myself! I might even hate my parents for forcing me into doing stuff I don't like!

"You know, it really wasn't my idea to be a doctor, anyway. My parents thought it would look good for the family if I became one. That way they could brag about me, not to mention themselves. You know, get more brownie points from friends and neighbors."

Ahgri asked, "What are your good passions, Jack? You must have a good passion?"

"I already told you—Ajax! Ajax was my one and only passion in life. I loved my horse so much. My mother took her away from me! After she was gone, I hated myself because I didn't intervene to stop the killing of Ajax! I got counseling for many years to deal with that trauma. They labeled me with PTSD, Ahgri! I have PTSD because my horse was killed by my mother! Isn't that pretty freakin' weird? Whose mom kills their son's pet and best friend?

"Believe me, I have tried to get over it, and I think I'm doing a pretty good job. I think Dixon is helping me. I know it sounds strange, but I think I am a passionate man, and now I have a new passion—helping her."

"Yes, Miss Dixon is correct. You must have a purpose. Go back to the days of Ajax when she was alive. Get that feeling of zest and vigor back. You cannot continue to be hateful and sad for something that happened tragically when you were a child. At some point, you must snap out of it!" Ahgri snapped his fingers. "You must remember, our paths in life are never straight lines. We climb to the summit in a zigzag manner, never straight up the mountain. We call that technique switchbacking. Many times, we go around boulders or even travel back down the mountain before we go back up again. Ajax was a straight and true path for you until she broke her leg. Then it became a boulder that hit you. Sometimes that happens, too. But now is the time that you need to get up, my friend, and maybe even find a new, fresh path. You cannot swim in your miseries forever, Jack. You will certainly drown, my friend!"

Ahgri sat up straighter. "Try to make your life more than just a word—more than a paragraph. Why not have your life play out like a novel? Be a book, Jack! Yes! In fact, be a bestseller. Live life as if it's a beautiful story, full of love, passion, and meaning! Instead of using Ajax as your reason to be a mean, dispirited, and unlikable person, use her as your jumping-off point. Start over! You have a chance to come back to life, Jack. Reset yourself! Ajax was your passion, but now you have a new one. One that is in the moment. That would be your patient, Miss Dixon. She will save you, my friend.

"One other thing I want to tell you," said Ahgri. "Do you know that we have kinship, Jack? I knew this when we first became friends. My life started out in the jungles of Africa where it is dangerous, and thick foliage prevents you from seeing too far ahead. I have been climbing toward the summit all my life. I have not reached there yet, but I will. You, my friend, started your life on the top and now have rolled down to the jungles. You need to let go of your past and start climbing again. You need to reach the summit!

"I tell you these things because it is not easy to live your life, and it is quite hazardous to get to the very top. But when you do, you will see the beautiful sunrise. That is when you will know what real passion is. You will know that God exists, and life is beautiful! Only then will you be able to write that bestselling novel. I hope someday you get there, my friend."

Ahgri paused and sipped the abhorrent coffee. "Your life has been different. It is as if your parents have been dragging you up the mountains with ropes and you simply hang on and simply let them. I fear that one of these days, the ropes will break, and you will fall unless you learn to be your own man. You climb that mountain, Jack—don't let others climb it for you. Always focus on the journey. Find your own passion, and don't hang on to your parents' ropes."

Jack, expressionless, sat clutching every word his friend was saying. "Wow, Ahgri. Are you some kind of psychiatrist or something? I thought you were going into family practice."

"I am not a psychiatrist, Jack. I am your *rafiki*, your friend!

Once you find Bert, we could even have a little ceremony for them. I would even wear my best *shuka* for that event!"

"Come on, Ahgri, no one wants to see you wear one of those Maasai blankets! They'll just laugh at you!" he said, teasing his friend. "I think I'll tell Jones in the morning that I need to take a few days off. I'll start at Fort Knox. A military base just south of Louisville. They should have all the names of former soldiers, right? It's only about an hour's drive, and they'll tell me how to find this Bert guy. Then I'll contact him and bring him back! What do you think, Ahgri?"

He raised his hands, with palms facing upward. "It sounds very simple, but you do know that nothing is ever that easy. If it was, why would she not have done that, already? But life is certainly mysterious. I say *nenda kwa amani*—go in peace, my friend!"

31

Jack Maizel was ecstatic, but at the same time, he was nervous. He had gotten to the internal medicine floor earlier than he ever had because he wanted to tell Dr. Jones about his revelation and what his plans were to help Mildred and complete her wishes.

He didn't like Dr. Jones—actually he hated him because of his pompous and know-it-all attitude—but was also a bit intimidated by him. He knew Dr. Jones had more experience at being a doctor than he ever would, and Jack questioned whether that made him a compassionate doctor.

This morning, Jack was going to ask—no, tell—Dr. Jones that he wasn't going to be there the rest of the week because he needed to do a monumental task to help his patient, Miss Dixon. As he stared at the ceiling, thinking about what he would say to Dr. Jones, he heard a booming voice behind him.

"Wonders never cease, do they, Mr. Maizel?" said Dr. Jones.

Startled, Jack turned around and was surprised to see his attending physician on the floor so early. "Oh, Dr. Jones, I didn't know you were behind me. Good morning, sir."

Dr. Jones looked at him suspiciously. "You seem to be in a good mood and not too ornery yet. Too early for you, Mr. Maizel? So, let's get to the point of why you are here so early. What's on your mind? I assume you have a question for me that I probably won't be answering favorably. But go ahead. I admire your courage this morning."

"Well, Dr. Jones, it's about Miss Dixon. Look, she's dying, and there is nothing we can do for her, correct? It's just not right to try all the song and dance we always do for terminal patients so that we can make ourselves feel better. If you do a deep dive into our feelings, you know, we're not really wanting to help them. It's about us making ourselves feel like we're doing something good. You know we're not, and they are miserable while we experiment on them. It's just not right, Dr. Jones. They live a horrible life of chronic nausea, hair loss, and just not feeling well and then die soon. Their quality of life becomes horrific. It's a blur to them!

"Miss Dixon has no family. She is going to die and has one man who she has loved all her life. His name is Bert Vines. She told me this! She wants to see him one last time before she goes to God. Why not, right? Why shouldn't she have this? I want to help her and find Bert to reunite them. Then, I want her to go to her own house to see her own things and lie on her own bed and smell familiar scents. That's important! Let her die at home in familiar surroundings. Let's not let her die in the hospital . . . an institution with strangers around. She wants to live her last days at home, Dr. Jones. At peace and surrounded by her stuff—pictures, blankets, dishes—just her stuff! I want to go find him, Dr. Jones. I want to do this for Dixon before she dies." Jack straightened his posture and with confidence, as if he was determined to go on a mission, looked directly into Dr. Jones's eyes and said, "I am asking for a few days off—a week would be great. Can I have one week off from my rotation, sir?"

Jack didn't know that his rounding group had gathered around behind him. They started to clap, then whoop and holler. Then in unison they chanted, "Go Jack, go Jack, go Jack!" He was surprised and a bit embarrassed.

Dr. Jones's facial expression did not change. He made direct eye contact with Jack, but Jack didn't budge.

"Mr. Maizel, I appreciate your passionate speech," said Dr. Jones. "Yes, she is terminal, and yes, we are willing to send her home, but she needs end care and support. It would be incredibly irresponsible on the part of our medical profession to send her home without that. We have our social workers working on placement. There are a couple of hospice centers here in town, but your patient does not want to go there. I already asked her.

"Part of the problem with sending her home is that she lives in such a rural area it is difficult to have regular hospice care and quick access to a hospital in case she bleeds out or has any complications from the cancer. A big problem for her is that since her liver is virtually nonfunctional because of the cancer, her protein production and the anticoagulant systems are shot. Therefore, she is at tremendous risk for sudden bleeds. We cannot let her bleed to death in her own home. That would be irresponsible. As physicians, it is still our responsibility to give her the best medical attention until she passes on."

Dr. Jones then gave a slight nod to Jack. He looked at Ahgri and said, "Mr. Zuri, I want you to take over Mr. Maizel's patients while he is gone for a few days. He will be back on Monday, the twentieth."

"Thirty days hath September," Jack said softly.

"What's that, Mr. Maizel? What did you say?"

"I said thirty days hath September, Dr. Jones. It's an old grade school poem for remembering the number of days in our months."

Dr. Jones looked puzzled. "So what are you saying, Mr. Maizel? You want until September thirtieth to complete your mission?"

"No, sir, I was just repeating something Dixon told me. I think my goal is to find Bert by the twentieth! That's all."

"Okay, Mr. Maizel! Then go, be on your way! Find Bert and be back by next week! You are excused until the twentieth. You may go!"

Jack smiled and started to trot down the hallway. He made a bit of a howling sound as he left. His fellow rounding buddies, who'd been listening to the entire exchange, cheered and clapped. They patted his back as he headed toward the exit.

"Mr. Maizel!" yelled Dr. Jones.

Jack stopped and pensively turned around. "Yes, Dr. Jones?"

Dr. Jones smiled and said, "Godspeed! Godspeed to you, Mr. Maizel. Go find Mr. Bert!"

Jack smiled, made a whooping noise, and then ran out as fast as he could.

32

Specialist 4 Edmond Hill handed over a pile of forms and said, "Fill these pages out, sir, and I'll submit them for processing."

As he leafed through the pages, Jack Maizel said, "Look, Hill, I'm not a relative . . . I'm just looking for an old guy that a patient wants to see before she dies. I don't know how to answer all the details that you want here, so there's no way I can fill these out!"

"Sir," replied Hill. "First, you may address me as Spec 4 Hill and not just Hill, sir. Second, it does not matter whether you are a relative or not—we need to follow the rules. Anyone asking for information and records for military service members, past or present, must complete these forms. I will get you started. Is that a B-U-R-T or B-E-R-T? And is that his first name in full? Is it short for something like Bertram or Norbert? Or is it Burton?"

"Come on, Hill, I don't know. I was just told his name is Bert Vines. I just assumed it was spelled with a B-E and not a B-U. I guess I don't really know. As far as these forms go, there's gotta be over twenty pages of questions here, and I don't much feel like taking some sort of exam just now! I don't know one thing about this man except he's pretty old—mid-sixties—and his name is Bert Vines. He served in the Army

Air Forces during World War II and came back to eastern Kentucky right after the war. Then he kind of disappeared.

"I'm taking care of a lady patient at a hospital who's dying, and she wants to see him before she does. The man, like I said, is older and he was on one of those bombing planes during the war. Flew into Germany a few times, the lady told me. He lost an arm and had some disfigurement of his face. Can't you just look him up in some kind of log and find out where he is? I mean, he must be getting some kind of military payout, right? You guys pay for everything that happens to these war guys, don't you?"

The military clerk, appearing annoyed and not looking at Jack, shuffled some files and papers around as if he was looking for something. "Sir, are you a doctor? If so, I will ask my sergeant to assist you."

"Yeah, yeah, I'm a doctor all right! So, get me some better help than what you can give me please, Spec! Okay?"

"Yes, sir!" Specialist 4 Hill saluted him half-heartedly but with obvious disdain and picked up the phone.

*   *   *

An overweight man, Staff Sergeant Ollie Cross, sat at his desk, making no attempt to rise from his seat. He wore a masklike face with no signs of emotion and appeared bored while stacking papers on one corner of his desk. Nearing retirement, three months left, he did not want to be there and despised the man—a kid, in his mind—who stood a few feet before him.

This punk is arrogant and obviously has no discipline or control over his actions, thought Cross as Jack explained his situation once again. *What is this kid up to? Looking for some ex-military man from World War II of all things? Helping some elderly woman? I don't think so! Must be working for a PI. That's weird*, he thought.

"So, let me get this straight," the sergeant said. "You say you're a doctor, right, and you wanna know about some ex-military man named Bert V.?"

"Yes, Vines is his last name. I want to know where this man is, please. I don't understand why that would be so difficult for you to just tell me." Jack was irritated and short-tempered. "I'm sorry, but everyone here is acting like they're brain dead. I'm frustrated. I need help, please. Doesn't the army or the government send Vines money every month for getting hurt on the job? You know, like some type of compensation?"

"Look, young man!" Cross suddenly stood. "First, I don't believe you're a damn doctor. You're nothin' but a punk kid, the way I see it. And second, if you want information, you need to feed us some fuel! What's his full name? You know, the name he was given by his parents? Where did Vines serve? Was he an NCO? An officer? What was his highest attained rank? What year did he enlist and what years did he serve? Where did he do his basic? His tour? You said he was in the Army Air Forces during the war, right? Okay, what was his assignment? Mechanic? Pilot? Navigator? What squadron? What bomber group? Was he in Europe or Asia? You need to help us out, son! That's why you gotta fill out the fricking forms, kid! Got it?"

Cross imagined he was all red in the face now and could feel a pounding headache coming on. "And another thing . . . what you said about getting paid for getting hurt! That's just plain disrespectful! This soldier, from what you're telling me, was hurt fighting for our country, and you're making it sound like he just had any old job—digging trenches or something—and accidentally hit his leg with a pickax, got hurt, and now gets disability. We take care of our combatants and veterans. They put their lives in harm's way for all of us! That's just not the way it works, kid! You need to grow up and become a part of the real world—hardships, pain, and suffering. You don't always get paid to get hurt."

"Okay, okay! I'm sorry, Sarge. Calm down, please," said Jack, a little intimidated by the burly man. He tried to get a better grip on himself.

Sergeant Cross took in a deep breath, then exhaled loudly and slowly shook his head. He sat back down. "Do you know about the St. Louis fire of 1973?"

"No, what fire?"

"On July 12, 1973, millions of military records at the NPRC—
that's the National Personnel Records Center, if you don't know—were
destroyed by a large fire. Yeah, the military records from around 1912
through 1964 were mostly destroyed. Their military discharge information all went up in smoke! You know—poof!" he said as he put
both hands up with palms up. "Burned to a crisp, as they say! The
records that were salvaged had irreversible water damage and many
could hardly be read."

Cross wiped the small beads of sweat that were forming on his
forehead. He became excited as he continued to talk about the fire. "It
was a disaster, all right. You had all kinds of people blaming each other
for their stupidity that let this valuable information be destroyed. It
took a couple of days to put out that fire. So much information about
our military heroes was just wiped out. Lots of people were mad. Even
had a congressional hearing. But as usual nothing came of it. They
eventually built a brand-new building. You know—like it was going to
solve the problems!"

"Look, Mr. Sergeant Cross, I don't really care about this fire in St.
Louis all those years ago. I just want to know about Bert Vines."

"I'm telling you all this because the records for Vines may not even
be available because of this fire!" Sergeant Cross said. "You may end
up in many dead-end spots. But I do get a bit carried away about the
fire. That was a historic fire, and let's face it, how many historic fires are
there? Of course, there was the New York fire of 1776 or the Chicago,
Wisconsin, and Michigan fires of 1871. And, how about the—"

"Please, Sergeant Cross! I don't need your tangential speech about
fires. You're talking a lot of nonsense here. I am simply here to find out
how to find a person who was a former military man from World War
II. It's simple. That's all I want to know."

Fire stories were always fascinating, even mesmerizing to Sergeant
Cross. It excited him to talk about it but also calmed him down. "Sorry
about that, young man! I get carried away with fires. They are interesting to me. So, what's his full name again?"

Jack sighed and repeated the only information he had.

After another hour of rambling conversations about the weather, lakes, Native Americans, and bomber planes, the sergeant found a file on Sergeant First Class Burt G. Vines.

"Now this file wasn't housed in St. Louis. This one was always here because he retired from Fort Knox. The file says Sergeant Vines had an honorable discharge in 1978. His forwarding address is Rural Route #5 in Benton, Kentucky. Says here, he works and lives on a Boy Scout reservation. The Four Rivers Boy Scout Reservation near the town of Fairdealing, with headquarters in Paducah. Want it?"

Jack thought for a moment. "That can't be right! Vines was in the war in the 1940s. This can't be the same man."

"Well, I don't know, but that's what this says, kid. Take it or leave it, suits me fine either way. Want the information or not?"

Jack took the records from the military man and scanned it rapidly with his tired eyes. After a few minutes of reading through it, he said, "This can't be the same man, but I'll go there and question him. Maybe he's a son or some other relative."

Thanking the military man for his help, Jack walked out with notes he had taken from the records.

* * *

Jack, upset with his difficulties obtaining information, sat in his car for a moment trying to determine his next move. He realized he was not fully prepared for his sleuth adventure. He would need to go back and get more information from Mildred.

Just then, a sharp tap at the driver's side window snapped him out of his contemplations.

"Hey, kid, roll down your window!" the man shouted.

"Yes, what is it, Sergeant Cross?"

"Look, I was hard on you in there, kid, because I didn't like you much when you first walked in. It's your arrogance, buddy! You got too much of it. It's distasteful, and you turn people off. It's not really what you say, but how you say it. You understand me, kid? Just soften up a little, and you'll get honey instead of vinegar, okay? Anyway, I got to thinking when you left my office. What if this kid is really trying to help an elderly lady to reconnect with her man? It would be nice if they got together. So, I'm gonna give you some advice. Vines is a common name, as you know. I don't think this is the guy you're looking for. Yeah, he probably knows someone who may know the guy you're really looking for—maybe it's a long-lost cousin or other relative! Who knows! It's worth a try, but my advice is get in contact with a guy by the name of Pfister. Marcus Pfister. He's a private eye, former college football star and combat veteran who lives in Elizabethtown. He'll do you right! The man can fish a dead skunk out of a garbage dump even if you got smelling problems, from what I hear. Okay, that may not be hard to do, but the guy helps relatives and friends find lost ones. He's good and local. He might charge you a good penny, but I think you'll find your man with Mr. Pfister. I jotted down his name and number if you want it.

"Hang in there, kid. I hope you find Vines. I think it's great that you're helping some old lady find her past! To get to the Boy Scout camp, just drive down toward Elizabethtown on 31 West, then get on the Western Kentucky Parkway. You'll drive a couple of hours. Find your way to LBL—that's Land Between the Lakes—and stay there for the night. They got a bunch of little hotels by Kentucky Lake. Then get directions from gas stations to the Boy Scout reservation.

"If you want Pfister, go to Elizabethtown and find Deckard School Road toward Vine Grove. Good luck, kid!"

Jack Maizel sat there for a few moments, then smiled. For the first time in his life, he felt that he was doing something worthy. Someone took him seriously and tried to help. It felt pretty good.

33

Even though his car windows were rolled up tight, Jack Maizel had difficulty taking anything but shallow breaths because of the dense dust stirred up from the gravel road. There was a long procession of cars in front and behind him, all traveling at a steady rate of about fifteen miles per hour. A few signs on the highway had indicated there was some type of camporee going on this weekend. He didn't know what a camporee was but assumed it was an event where a bunch of scouts were going to camp out.

As he followed the procession, he thought about turning around when, out of nowhere, he came upon a house. It was a small ranch home with rust stains on the white clapboard and a partial front façade made of river rocks. It was obvious even from the road that the house had been barraged by thick dust from the gravel road for years, as everything had a grayish coating on its surface. Even the front lawn had a gray-white cast, almost obscuring the green grass.

He pulled into the gravel driveway where a vintage—probably a WWII-era—jeep was parked at one end. The other vehicles that trailed Jack continued straight. Making way to the front door, he spied a small torn notebook paper that was taped to the door. It simply declared, "DOWN THE HILL." Just below that, "Sarge" was scribbled.

What does this mean? What hill? thought Jack. *Is "Sarge" actually Sergeant Burt Vines, the man Sergeant Cross told me about?*

He looked around the property for any signs of life, then walked toward the jeep. It appeared very old and looked like the ones he'd seen in war movies as a kid. He then followed the gravel road, and saw that it took a sharp downward grade just past the house. *This must be the hill*, he thought and got back in his car.

The gravel road leading down the hill made a natural left bend, where it took him to a broad open field ending at the shoreline of a large lake. In the center of the field, there was a solitary raised concrete-block grilling pit. The pit was at least one hundred feet long and about four feet wide with the walls on either side of the pit rising about two and half feet from ground level. Multiple grill grates, about three feet wide, straddled both edges of the wall and spanned the entire length of the pit.

Jack got out of his car to see if he could find anyone. *Good thing I got shorts and a T-shirt on. It sure is hot here! The hat helps, too!* Jack thought. *Where are all the cars that traveled here?* he wondered.

A man with the dirtiest overalls Jack had ever seen rose from behind part of the pit wall. "Hey, are you my replacement help?" he shouted in a Southern drawl. "Mr. Johns send ya?"

Startled, Jack didn't respond immediately. He didn't know what the man was referring to. Without waiting for a reply, the man pointed to a small building.

"You ain't dressed right to be doing any cook'n' these birds with me and the skeeters are gonna take a hunk out of you when they start bit'n', so slip on some coveralls I got hang'n' in that shed yonder. Then take that rusted jeep, over yonder, and git me some more wood from the log pile behind that pole barn. If there ain't any or 'nough of 'em already split, go 'head and crack 'em for me. I've got all kinda axes all over the place—just fetch one for yourself. Bring 'em down to me right fast 'cause I need to git this here fire goin' before I lose the hot tinders."

Not sure how to respond or know what to say, Jack started to speak, but the man kept yelling. "What're ya wait'n' fer? Now, get a move on it, son!"

Shrugging and realizing it wasn't worth an explanation right now as the man was trying to start a huge fire in the grill pit, Jack walked over to the vintage jeep and got in. He had no idea how to drive it since it was a manual shift. He sat there for a moment and the man yelled out again. "What the hell you doin', kid? I need that wood now, not t'morrow!"

Jack almost yelled back to tell him that he couldn't drive this thing, but he let his natural instincts take over and managed to start it. He had seen enough war movies and other television shows to have an idea of how manual transmission shifting worked on a jeep. He started moving, but it kept buckling and stopping as his timing with the clutch and gear drive couldn't quite get coordinated. He finally made it to the pole barn, found some split logs, loaded them into the jeep, and made his way back to the firepit.

Jack tried to introduce himself to the man with the filthy overalls, but the man paid no attention to him. He was so intent on getting the pit fires ready that he didn't even say hi.

Not knowing what to do, Jack decided to become the man's assistant and help him out so he could talk with him later. He assumed this was the former Sergeant Vines.

As Jack and the dirty overalls man built an enormous fire in the firepit, kids in Boy Scout uniforms and a few adult scoutmasters started to make their way to the grounds around the pit. The man said, "Okay, we gotta put them thar birds on the grill now or they gonna bolt." He laughed.

Chicken, stored in boxes and sliced in half, was placed on the large grill grates, which held about a half dozen each. Another grate went on top so that Jack and the man could walk from one end of the pit to the other to baste the chicken with an aromatic-smelling barbecue sauce.

They proceeded to turn the chicken over by grabbing the handles of the grate protruding from either side of the pit. This process was continued until every grate was flipped along the length of the firepit. They then walked back to the head and did it again until the barbecued chicken was cooked exactly right to the specifications of the man.

This routine continued all afternoon as crowds of people got larger until about 5 p.m., when there was a sudden pause in the noise. Despite the shorts and T-shirt Jack was wearing, he was sweaty and dirty from the nonstop work.

A man with a Boy Scout uniform made a peace sign with the first two fingers of his right hand. The hush was sudden and immediate as the man said a prayer. Suddenly, the chatter revved up again while everyone made their way to get a plate full of barbecued chicken, a bag of potato chips, a small Styrofoam cup of coleslaw, and a scoop of vanilla ice cream.

Serving the scouts for three straight hours, Jack kept the fire going and added more chicken when they ran out and kept serving the food to the hungry scouts. Although exhausted from the lifting, serving, and heat, Jack felt invigorated to do manual labor. It was fun to see the kids eat the food he was preparing for them.

Having looked for a lull in the activities all evening, Jack was eager to approach the dirty overalls man and inquire about Bert Vines. Could the dirty overalls man actually be Sergeant Vines, the man Cross told him about? *As soon as I can get a short break, I'll ask him. In the mean-time, I'll just keep feeding these hungry boys. It's kinda fun.*

34

About an hour later as Jack and the dirty overalls man were cleaning up and the quiet consumed the evening, a group of boys abruptly emerged from near the lake area, shouting and trotting toward the grill pits, breaking the tediousness of Jack's tasks.

Behind the yelling and shouting boys were two adult scoutmasters who were carrying a small boy on a makeshift stretcher. One of the scoutmasters yelled out, "Sarge, call an ambulance! Call them now! He's fix'n' to die if we don't get him some help now!"

The other said, "Steve's hurt bad. He's gonna die if we don't get a doctor or someone here right away!"

Jack, without hesitation, ran over and started assessing the boy. "Someone tell me what happened!"

An adult scoutmaster named Phil asked, "Who are you, young man?"

"I'm Jack Maizel. I have some medical training and may be able to help."

"Okay, sure. Steve, here, and some of the other boys were rough-housing over by the lake just before dinner. He fell and hit his head hard on a rock sticking out of the water. He passed out for a couple of minutes but then came back around pretty quickly. There was a small cut on the side of his head, so we stopped the bleeding by putting some pressure over it and applied a small dressing to cover it. Steve told us that he had a bit of a headache but felt pretty good otherwise. He went back to doing normal boy stuff with his friends and later we came over here for dinner.

"About an hour later, Steve started to complain of a bad headache and threw up a couple of times. Then he kinda started breathing real funny. Next thing you know, he passed out! A couple of the boys who know CPR started on him. I told them to stop because he was still breathing, and he had a decent pulse—that wasn't his problem! But, no matter what we did, he just wouldn't respond! That's why we brought him up here. I think we ought to get him to a hospital right away!"

Jack asked for a flashlight from one of the boys and saw that the right pupil was slightly enlarged and not responsive to the bright light he shined over it. The left was a bit sluggish to react but was responsive.

Taking a deep breath to try to stay calm, Jack pulled the boy's shoes and socks off, then formed a sort of hitchhiker's thumb with his right hand and swooped it up the boy's feet, starting with the heels. Steve's big toe raised up toward his head and the little toes flailed outwardly.

"Positive Babinski's," whispered Jack to no one in particular.

He immediately turned around and asked the sergeant to get him a power drill with at least a half-inch bit along with a sharp knife, scissors, and a razor. "Get me some rubbing alcohol and cotton balls or gauze, too. Sterile, if you can find them!"

"What in tarnation are you gonna do, son?" said the sergeant.

"This boy has a bleed in his head; probably a subdural or epidural hematoma has formed. The clot and blood need to be evacuated right away, or it'll push his brain down through a hole at the base of the skull. That'll cause an uncal herniation of the brain, and he could die. Only way to relieve the pressure is to drill a couple of holes in his head! Burr holes to see if we can get the clot and excess blood accumulation out!"

The group stared at him, not able to comprehend a word Jack said.

Jack breathed out and said, "We can't let him die!"

A large group now formed around the boy, who was lying on the stretcher, now on the ground. "Okay, everyone, take at least three steps back," ordered Jack. "I need one of you scouts to assist me, too."

Steve, the injured boy, breathed shallowly, still unconscious.

"Did someone call the ambulance?" Jack asked.

"Yup, I called 'em," said the sergeant, "but they said they'd be about forty-five minutes to get here."

"Did you tell them we have an extremely bad situation here?"

The sergeant just nodded, as if not knowing what to say.

"Okay, I have no choice, I've got to do this now! Where's my stuff that I asked for?"

One of the boys handed him an electric drill that required an extension cord to plug into the outdoor electrical box near the pit. Phil, the scoutmaster, had gathered other materials from the first aid kits that some of the boys had with them.

Jack had no time to think about the horrific situation he was in. He knew he had no backup like an attending physician to intervene in case he messed up. Jack was on his own.

He was scared and could feel his heart pounding hard and furious as he started to prepare for the emergency procedure. It reminded him of a similar situation he had while doing an elective rotation in neurosurgery. He got to the emergency room where a man came in with a head injury. The initial assessment was that he had a subdural bleed from trauma to the middle meningeal artery. The treatment was to immediately drill burr holes into his skull. He knew that but froze when one of the attendings pushed him away and took over.

For some reason, he felt more confident now. He had no choice. Was it standing his ground to the likes of Dr. Jones that gave him newfound courage? Or his rediscovery of passion, orchestrated by Dixon and Ahgri? He didn't know, but he knew he had to act right away or the boy was going to die. Soon!

I've never actually done this before. How did I get myself into this? Don't think, Maizel, just do it. You already know how to do this procedure. Just do it!

Someone had a small bottle of isopropyl alcohol, so he emptied about a third of it and filled it back to the top with water from a nearby well pump. He knew this mixture was much better at killing surface bacteria and viruses than the pure form. He poured the mixture over the knife blade and drill bit. He then took the razor and shaved the boy's hair just around the laceration and a couple of centimeters below the injury. He kept palpating the skull to feel the fracture line, but it was faint. He then inserted the knife edge just below what he felt was the fracture line, into the surface of the scalp, and made a deep slit until he hit the bone. One of the scouts had packs of gauze that he was using to soak up the bleeding.

He then took the variable speed drill and slowly entered the skull just below the fracture line, which was obvious now. After a moment of slow drilling, a burst of blood started to pour out.

It looks like I just pricked a water balloon, thought Jack. He then drilled another hole nearby and got even more blood.

The boy started to move, but Phil, the scoutmaster, kept firm hands on the boy's head and kept it stationary. Steve opened his eyes for a moment but closed them right away.

Jack reassessed his patient after letting the excess blood drain, then placed a thick gauze dressing over the burr holes. Steve's respirations seemed to be more regular and less shallow now. He knew the boy was still in danger and needed to be seen by a neurosurgeon as quickly as possible. But for now, he did everything humanly possible to save this boy's life, and deep inside, he knew he had done that. He was still frightened out of his wits, but he was relieved and elated at the same time. *Wow*, he thought, *I think I saved this boy's life!*

* * *

Faint sirens grew louder quickly. Everyone stared expectantly toward the gravel road sloping down the long hill.

Phil had stationed some of his boys at various parts of the winding road to help direct the ambulance. The EMTs pulled up near the large firepit, rushed toward the crowd of boys, and took over the situation.

"Who is in charge here? We need to know the history," exclaimed a female EMT with the name tag of "Molly" on her uniform.

The scouts all looked toward Jack Maizel, who was standing just a few feet away so as to be out of the way of the paramedic activities.

"Eleven-year-old male by the name of Steve," said Jack. "I don't know his last name, I'm sorry, who sustained a head injury approximately three hours ago. Reportedly, he lost consciousness but then experienced a period of lucidity followed by a progressive decline in consciousness and neurologic function that was noted to be associated with changes in respirations.

"Upon my initial examination, the boy was noted to be in an unconscious state. A linear laceration was found in the mid-right temporal area and a palpable linear ridge on the skull just below the laceration mark. The ipsilateral right pupil was noted to be dilated and not responsive to light while the left pupil was reactive but slightly sluggish to reaction. I performed a brief neuro exam, where I noted his reflexes were slightly hyperreflexive. He also had bilateral positive Babinski signs.

"I assessed him to have either a subdural or epidural bleed and felt he needed immediate evacuation of the hematoma and blood to relieve the cerebral pressures he was experiencing.

"I proceeded to create a burr hole, under less-than-ideal antiseptic conditions, just under the point of injury in an attempt to relieve the pressure. Blood with clotting elements were expelled from the hole. A second hole was drilled parallel to the first one. More blood and clots were drained. I'd say probably about thirty to forty-five cc's. I didn't have any suction devices or other instruments to aid in the removal of the clot, so I just depended on gravity and intracranial pressures to evacuate the blood as much as possible. As the drainage slowed, I placed a dressing over the wound and then you arrived."

After he finished his narrative, the boys, scoutmasters, and the sergeant were in awe listening to this young man. *Who is he?* they all wondered.

Molly, who had been furiously writing notes as Jack spoke, looked up and asked, "Are you a physician, sir?" Jack was taken aback because no one had ever seriously asked him if he was a physician. No one had ever called him sir, either. He always demanded that people call him *doctor* and they would either just roll their eyes or completely ignore him.

"Well, I'm just a medical student, but I saw this procedure done out in the field when I was on a neuro rotation a few months back."

Molly shook her head in amazement. "You are an amazing man with amazing skills. You will be a truly incredible doctor. I would be proud to call you my doctor when you start your own practice, sir!"

The EMTs worked to stabilize the child, starting an IV for medication access and oxygen by nasal canula; they then placed him on a gurney and maneuvered him into place to transport him into the ambulance.

Molly walked over just as they were leaving and said, "Doctor, I want to shake your hand. I believe you saved this young man's life. You certainly have God's given gift of healing your fellow human beings. I am proud to know you, sir!"

They sped away with lights and sirens while raising a thick cloud of dust, which was magnified by the headlights of the vehicle. Jack Maizel, watching the ambulance pull away and musing over what Molly just said to him, smiled and shook his head slightly as he stared at the congregation of people that surrounded him.

As the flashing lights faded, the entire band of more than two hundred boys turned their attention toward Jack and began clapping, whistling, and cheering.

Stunned by the outburst, he was suddenly overwhelmed with emotion. With a loss of words, he kept trying but failing to keep his face dry, despite constantly dabbing his eyes with his shirt sleeves. The boys lined up and, one by one, walked up to him, patted him on the back, and said thank you.

This is the second time in the past few days that a group of people clapped and cheered for me for doing something good to help others, he thought. He was acknowledged for being someone important. Yes, he was happy!

35

Despite overwhelming exhaustion, Jack Maizel had a fitful night of rest. Snippets of dreams startled him awake most of the night while damp bedsheets from sweat made it even more difficult to get comfortable. He was not able to recall all the details but knew the dreams had to do with him drilling into a boy's head. *How horrific the noise of the drill was*, he thought, *but lifesaving!*

The morning light was breaking into the room as he lay awake. He wondered, *How the hell did I do that? Where did that even come from? Now, they're calling me a hero. It feels good, but did I really save that boy's life? What if I hit something in his brain that's going to cause damage to him in some way for the rest of his life?*

His mind drifted to the events after the boy was taken away in the ambulance. A bit of whooping and hollering from joyous but tired boys followed by a solemn prayer for their fellow scout. Despite their exhaustion after a long day, conversations continued about the medical drama they all witnessed that resulted in a miracle. Someone even called the hospital from a nearby pay phone later, but all they would tell him was the boy was in stable condition after emergency surgery. Before everyone turned in for the night, Jack and the dirty overalls man finally made formal self-introductions. Just as Jack suspected, the man was indeed Sergeant Vines, also known as Sarge. Jack told him who he was looking for and why. Since both men were overwhelmingly exhausted, Sergeant Vines proposed to take Jack to a nearby motel where they could meet up for breakfast the next morning and talk about Jack's search.

* * *

As Jack walked into the attached diner of the motel, Sergeant Vines hollered, "Hey, Dr. Jack, over here!" Jack saw him waving to him to sit with him, and he made his way over to the table.

"Good morning, Sergeant Vines. Sorry I'm late; I slept in a bit longer than I anticipated."

"Are you kidd'n', doc! You deserve to sleep the whole day if you want! Why, after barbecu'n' all those chickens and serv'n' 'em kids all afternoon, then sav'n' that boy's life, you deserve to be in one of those king-size motel beds. Maybe even one of them vibrat'n' kinds!" He snickered.

"Thanks!" Jack replied with a broad smile.

"Let's order some breakfast and get some coffee in us and we can talk 'bout what you came up here fer. By the way, I called the hospital this mornin' and that Steve kid is gonna be just fine. Good as new, they said! They told me that you did a darn good job, and he wouldn't be livin' if you didn't do what you did fer 'im! Now, that's gotta make you feel real good, right? We're all mighty proud of what you done, doc!"

Jack just smiled and shook his head a bit, then proceeded to give his order to the pretty waitress.

Jack started the conversation by addressing the man as Sergeant Vines. The other man immediately put his hand up to stop him from saying any more. "Listen, they called me that, but now they just call'n me Sarge. I retired a few years ago, but I can't shake that military label off me. Don't really like it since I just wanna be called mister, but I guess that's life, huh?"

"Well, Mr. Vines, I'm looking for a man named Bert Vines. Even though you share the same last name, I don't think you are the man I'm looking for. You see, the Vines I need to find was in World War II. That makes you way too young to be him!"

The ex-military man laughed and said, "It's been a long time since anyone said somethin' good about me, like say'n' I'm young, so I'm tak'n' that as a compliment.

"You know," Vines continued, "I think you may be look'n' for a distant cousin of mine. You see the family came to this country and settled down in the Louisville area a few generations ago. Somewhere along the way, they all split up and went on to different parts of the country. Some stayed here in Kentucky and others went on yonder as far as Calee-fornia.

"I think that's who you're look'n' fer, doc. Probably one of them Calee-fornia cousins. There was a fourth or maybe a fifth cousin livin' out there around that time. A fella that had the same name as me. He was kinda a hero in the family because he was an officer and flew one of those big birds called a B-17. I'm bad at rememberin' names sometimes, but I think his name was Elbert or Gilbert, but he didn't go by Bert. I think he might have used the family's original I-talian name of Vinelli. So, you ought to try that name, too, when you look fer this fella!"

Jack had just put a bite of omelet in his mouth and almost choked when Vines mentioned the name change.

"Wait! You mean people in your family actually changed their last names from the original? You know, I think Mildred, my patient, mentioned something about that. I need to go back and ask her!"

"Yeah, many of our family members, I reckon, did that. It was kinda a way fer sound'n' more American, you know chang'n' our I-talian names and mak'n' it more American. But, later, a bunch of our family people wanted to change it back to I-talian! His first name may have been Bert, Gilbert, or Elbert. His last name could've changed back to Vinelli.

"Yeah, like I said, I heard he was in one of those big warplanes. The B-17s! But we all lost touch with each other. I'm not sure what happened to him. I heard—but I ain't real sure if it's right—that he got shot up pretty bad. He managed to come back and settle down somewhere in eastern Kentucky with a gal named Mildred. She was his fiancée before he left for Europe—a nurse and a pretty good lookin' one from what I heard!"

"Mister Vines, I appreciate this information a lot, but can you tell me when the last time you heard from or about him was? And do you happen to know what his rank was in the Army Air Forces?"

"Like I said, doc, we all lost touch with each other. The last time we heard anything was when we thought he came back to Kentucky. Truthfully, we really didn't know if he came back dead or livin'. I reckon the man was livin', though. I know he was a first lieutenant. No one in the Vinelli family ever got too far in school and stuff, but I heard he was real smart. He was an air cadet before the war and even went to college. He was gonna be an architect, I think. He was gonna fly one of those big birds, but when he enlisted, they wanted him to be a bombardier on account of him being so good in arithmetic! Those fellas had to be real smart to use that complicated Nord'n bombsight!

"Yup, we're all proud of someone like him being a family member and all—he really was a hero, but no one kept in touch much those days! I'd like to know what happened to him. I was expect'n' him to be governor or one of those slick politicians one of these days!"

Both men became quiet for a few moments.

"I think if you can find that fiancée of his, Mildred, then you should be able to find Bert. Ain't you think'n' that too?"

Jack replied, "I have found Mildred. She's a patient of mine and is dying. Her dying wish is to see Bert one last time. That's why I'm doing this. I want her to be together with her man before she passes."

"Well, I'll be! You're quite a fella, doc! A great doc that cares about the souls of patients! I seen ya in action last night. You could tell that you cared about the boy's soul, too. That's a sign of a great doc. Just amaz'n'!

"My best bet is for you to start look'n' in California. Probably in that San Diego area. If my memory's kinda right, I recall that a bunch of Vinellis and Vineses live around there. Big navy station, too. They call it—I'm a think'n' the Thirty-Second Street Naval Station. They might have records since military personnel from all branches can use things on the base like the commissary and the post exchange. Give them a holler and just tell 'em you're look'n for a World War II vet by the name of Gilbert or Elbert Vinelli . . . or it could be Bert Vines, too. Give 'em as much detail as you can, you know like he was a bombardier on a B-17 and whatever else you know 'bout him. They should be able to help ya!"

When they finished breakfast, Vines said, "Come on, I'll take you back to the reservation and the camp where you can get your car. If you want, you can come back here, take it easy, enjoy the lake, or hang out with me all day. The boys wanted you to be their guest of honor for dinner tonight. They'll do some skits and even sing'n' after dinner. They're always mak'n' pizzas on the firepit, too! It's purty yum-yum good!"

"I really need to get back to Lexington, but I'll see if I can get a little extra time so I can attend the dinner. That sounds good!"

"I know the boys'll get a kick at see'n' ya again!"

Jack was bothered by the possible name changes. *Who am I looking for?* he thought. *Bert Vinelli or Bert Vines? Could it be Elbert or Gilbert? Dixon called him Vines, but was it Burt or Bert? Did she tell me about the Vinelli name? I need to ask her about that, too! Maybe he's one of those that didn't change his name. . . . Surely Dixon would have told me if Bert had been a name-changer. First thing I need to do when I get back is to get this cleared up! I need to see Dixon right away!*

*   *   *

Jack spent much of the day with Vines, riding around in the vintage jeep and visiting the various boys' campsites. At each stop, the boys cheered Jack's arrival and surrounded him, asking questions and wanting him to sign autographs. Several boys asked about going into medical school. They were so impressed with his feat they looked at him as a hero and wanted to be like him.

Wow, he thought, *I actually had influence on some of the kids to go into medicine. Wait 'til Ahgri and Dixon hear about this. Jones'll have a shit fit!*

Later, a few of the boys wanted to take him out on a canoe ride to an island that was a Native American burial mound that ended up becoming an island after the Tennessee River was dammed to create Kentucky Lake in 1944. When they came upon it, Jack got out of the boat and immediately spotted an arrowhead. It was in near-perfect shape with a small piece of flint chipped in one corner. It felt good in his hands to rub the facets that made up its surface. He'd never seen one before and thought it was a good omen. It was just so cool to find history and touch it and feel it. Jack was thrilled.

That evening, the boys made the most delicious pizza in the open firepit. They were loaded with pepperoni, onions, peppers, mushrooms— almost every imaginable topping. Even anchovies!

Afterward the boys performed a skit they made up and called it "Dr. Jack, Our Hero!" It was the story of how the young medical student saved one of their fellow scouts by drilling a hole in the boy's skull with a regular hand drill.

The play also depicted a scene in the future where Steve, the boy who was saved, was now a scientist who found a cure for cancer and saved millions of people. But he knew that he would never have had the opportunity if it wasn't for Dr. Jack. So, with that one action by Dr. Jack, how much of humanity did he influence? Dr. Jack was a hero for not only the Boy Scouts who were there but also the entire world in the future. His actions saved countless lives into future generations.

Right after the skit, Vines made an important announcement. He said that the neurosurgeon called him and reported that Steve would be completely back to functioning as a scout in a week. He said that Dr. Maizel saved the boy's life. Everyone shouted, clapped, cheered, whooped, and hollered. They, all at once, picked up Jack Maizel, and he rode on their shoulders in front of the campfire. There, Phil, the scoutmaster, in a special ceremony, presented Jack Maizel an Eagle Scout badge, making him a lifetime honorary member of the Four Rivers Boy Scout Council.

"Steve wouldn't be alive if Mr. . . . I mean, Dr. Jack Maizel, here, never graced us with his presence," said Phil. "He was sent to us by the Almighty to save an eleven-year-old boy. Who knows what this boy is destined for? What greatness awaits him? Maybe he is to sire offspring who will one day change the world. Maybe Steve will change the world.

"It doesn't matter for now. What matters is that this man, Dr. Jack Maizel, gave a boy—a stranger to him—a chance at life because he had the courage to do something no one could possibly have done except for him. He is a hero to Steve, to me, and all of us. We pray that Jack Maizel will have a good and true life and will help many other people in his lifetime. He's been blessed with the God-given gift of healing.

"To honor him, I, as a representative of the Four Rivers Boy Scout Council, present this brave and courageous man with the Eagle Scout badge. The highest honor a scout can achieve! We love you, Dr. Jack Maizel!"

Jack, still overcome with emotion, could not help but cry shamelessly. This was the first time in his entire young life that he felt a part of some incredible force that had purpose toward a greater cause. He did not know what that purpose was, but he knew that no matter what, he was not the same person who left Lexington just a few days ago. He was returning as a man with a sense of purpose, mission, and passion. The passion and mission to find the man Mildred desperately wanted to see before she left this world.

He excused himself because he had to get back to Lexington that night, but he promised to come back every year to the camporee and visit with the boys.

As Jack drove back to Lexington, the smile never left his face. He kept looking at the Eagle Scout badge and the arrowhead clutched in his hand.

36

Although elated and still clutching the Eagle Scout badge, Jack was so tired he kept fighting the urge to doze off. He tried to keep his mind active by fantasizing about finding Bert and bringing him home to Miss Dixon. Oh, how she would be happy. He pulled off at the end of the Western Kentucky Parkway at Elizabethtown, where the Bluegrass Parkway began. Problem was, they weren't connected directly, and the town of Elizabethtown became the connector for the two parkways. So, it was a natural break for Jack. A great place to just get some food and rest. He spied a motel near a diner with its lights still on, so he just stopped there.

It wasn't hard to find a vacancy in the slightly run-down Towne Motel. The motel clerk, quite a friendly elderly man, said, "Welcome to the best in town, young fella! You picked the finest and friendliest!"

Jack, tired but a bit wired after the incredible experience he just had, replied with a slight snicker. "Thanks, but I didn't know there was another motel in town."

The man laughed. "There aren't none that are open now, young man! The joke's on you!"

After a bit of small talk, Jack asked if there was a pay phone he could use. Jack put a dime in and dialed a number. Soon the operator came on.

"How can I help you?"

"I'd like to make a collect call."

"I need your name, sir, and then please hold until I come back on with your intended party."

On the third ring a pleasant voice accepted the charges for a collect call. "UK ER, this is Doris speaking, how can I help you?"

"Hi, Dor! This is Jack Maizel. Hey, thanks for accepting the collect call; I'm out of town and have no spare change with me. I need to speak with Ahgri Zuri, please."

"Always in trouble, aren't you, Jack! I figured you were having some trouble when the operator asked if I would accept a collect call from you! You know you can buy something, then get change and put the change in the phone. Is it that you are just too lazy to do that, Jack, or do you just like bumming off people?"

When Jack didn't reply, there were a few seconds of silence.

"Let me see if I can find him. I just can't figure out why he even talks to you, Jack. He is such a nice young man, but you, I just don't know about you, Jack! You're what they call a rascal!"

There were a few more moments of silence.

"Hello, Jack, is it you?"

"Ahgri, yeah, it's me! How you been?"

"Doris told me it was you, but I didn't believe it! What are you doing calling me in the ER? You know we can't receive social calls here!"

"I know, I know. I'm calling you collect, and Dor was nice enough to accept the charges. I need you to call me from one of the hospital phones. I want to know how Dixon's doing, and I've got some things to tell you—like how I put burr holes in a kid's skull to relieve a subdural hematoma!"

"You did what? Are you serious? Wow. That's pretty remarkable, Jack. Is the kid okay?"

"Yeah, Ahgri. I think he's gonna be okay. The neurosurgeons say I saved his life! Can you believe that? I saved someone's life! Wow! But I've got to tell you, the most important thing is that the whole situation has been an epiphany for me! For the first time in my life, I did something worthwhile and saved someone's life. All these people, Ahgri, thanked me and patted me on the back as if I just made the game-winning touchdown at a football game. I finally had a sense of belonging. That I was worthy of doing something good. I may like this doctoring business after all, Ahgri.

"So, I had a realization tonight while driving to a motel in a place called Elizabethtown. I was crossing this big bridge that goes across Kentucky Lake and two songs came on the radio, back-to-back. The first was a song by John Fred and His Playboy Band. I can't remember the name of the song—'Judy' something. I think it was from the mid-sixties, remember when we were kids?"

"Jack, you forget, I am not from this country, and I do not know a lot of the past cultures and the many songs that define generations."

"Oh, yeah, sorry, Ahgri! I always think that I've known you forever and that we grew up together! Anyway, I listened to the words—it's kind of a weird song and doesn't make sense.

"Okay, okay, I know it's weird, but the way I interpreted it was that Judy was in a disguise by wearing these big glasses and no one really knew who she was or what she liked, but when she took them off, her real self came out!

"It's like those superheroes. They put a cowl on and suddenly no one knows who they are. They always become a crime fighter! It could work the other way, too; how about the superhero who disguises himself as a newspaper reporter, but his real self is a guy who can fly and take on all kinds of villains?"

"Okay, Jack, but what are you saying? You don't make very much sense to me."

"So, I feel that way, Ahgri! I feel like I finally took these big, clunky glasses off, and now I'm a different person. I'm the real me! The real Jack Maizel. I see and feel things differently. Ever since Dixon told me the mayor story and sent me to look for her boyfriend, I feel like I'm actually doing something worthwhile.

"The second song I heard is about a guy who got out of prison and he's a little afraid to come home because he may not be wanted by his girlfriend any longer. It's been three years, and he doesn't know if his girlfriend still loves him. So, he asks her to tie a yellow ribbon around the old oak tree if she still wants him. But if she doesn't, then she puts up no ribbons. When the bus he's riding is nearing his destination, he sees a bunch of yellow ribbons tied around the tree!

"I'm imagining that I'm coming home now, and maybe I'll be welcomed. Maybe I found my place in life. I know there won't be yellow ribbons when I get back, but I do feel like I'm coming home to be the doctor I should be! Does that make sense?"

"I'm glad to hear this news, Jack! It sounds as if you have possibly discovered yourself. Maybe you will be a doctor for the people instead of a plastic surgeon. That would be a noble career. Remember, it's always about self-respect, Jack. It is not always about how many people you helped but what impact and influence you had in others' lives, as well as your own. Did you do what you want to do?

"When I was a kid, my grandfather—I knew him just a little because I ended up in an orphanage—said to me, 'Always be who you are and not someone else's dream.' In other words, Jack, be who you are. Don't be what others want you to be. Be you, my friend! Maybe you've discovered who you are, Jack! Maybe you know who you are now! Maybe you will now be a happy man who is fulfilled!

"On another note, Jack, you asked about Miss Mildred, and I need to fill you in. I am afraid I have some disturbing news for you. On the day you left the hospital—last Tuesday morning—Miss Mildred started having some vague neurological symptoms. She seemed more confused and kept forgetting simple things, like her name, and then wanted to know when I was taking her out to dinner. At first, I thought she was joking, and I told her we would go to a local steak house—best steaks in town! But she didn't respond in the appropriate manner to a joke and appeared confused.

"Just this morning, she started having tremors in her hands that looked like flapping when she extended them out. Dr. Jones called it liver flapping. He explained to us, in rounds, that this is a result of a diseased and distressed liver. The blood was not being properly filtered out by the liver, which would normally remove toxins—in this case toxins that affect brain and neurological tissues. Therefore, the poisons that have settled in the brain are now causing a hepatic encephalopathy that exhibits numerous neurological symptoms. She is quite bedridden now, too. This has progressed very, very fast, Jack. I fear she does not have much longer."

Jack was stunned into silence. He didn't say anything for a long while; then Ahgri said, "Are you still there? Are you still with me, Jack?"

"Yeah! I just don't know what to say, Zuri. I gotta find Bert before it's too late! How is she doing right now?"

"She had a bad day, Jack. A really bad day today. She appears quite weak, and you could even say she is feeble. She cannot get out of bed without assistance at this time. Dr. Jones does not hold too much hope for her now."

"I'm tired, Zuri. I think I'll turn in for the night. I'll be there tomorrow morning bright and early. Right now, I'm overwhelmed. Good night."

"Usiku mwema—good night, Jack Maizel!"

After hanging up, Jack realized that in no way could he fall asleep now. He was so worried about Mildred Dixon that he immediately left the motel and drove back to Lexington.

37

After stopping at his apartment to shower, clean up, and grab a bite to eat, Jack Maizel immediately headed for Miss Dixon's room.

The hospital was abuzz with noises and activities as Jack walked quietly into the patient's room. He didn't want to disturb her in case she was asleep. He stood at her bedside for a while, assessing the grim situation. He was shocked at how much she had changed just since Tuesday—only four days ago! Her skin was so much more jaundiced now, and she appeared so thin, as if she had lost several pounds. *How could that be?* wondered Jack. *Can people turn for the worse that quickly?*

She suddenly fluttered her eyes open and looked at Jack. Slowly a smile formed in recognition. "Sonny Boy," she said groggily and quietly—almost a whisper. "I thought you'd never come back."

"Of course, I came back, Dixon! Looks like you got yourself into some trouble since I left you!" Jack said, gently and calmly, trying to hide his shock and not wanting to alarm her.

"I'm no good for nothing now. My mom kept saying that over and over when she was dying. That's just the way I feel. Rightly so, I think! I'm so weak and so tired. I can't remember too much, either. Something's wrong with my mind, Sonny Boy. I feel like I'm floating in space, and my mind is swimming in a deep pool of water. Not clear water but black water!

"Sometimes I hear things and other times I feel like I'm in another world. What's happening to me? I just want to go home. Remember, you told me I could go home if I had something bad. Well, I've got something bad now. Please drive me home. Will you take me home, please?"

"Okay, sure, I'll go get the car and take you home, Dixon!"

Jack realized that Mildred was not her usual self. She seemed agitated and a bit unsensible.

She slowly nodded, struggling to keep her eyes opened. Soon, a faint smile formed. "Where's Bert? Have you seen him? Did you find my Bert?"

"I'm close to finding him! I think he's in California, and I need to make a few phone calls. But don't you worry, Dixon. I'll find your man for you, and we're going to have a wedding right here in this room! I'm going to make that guy marry you. They call that a shotgun wedding, don't they? We'll do it up just right. I'll even get some of those Hot Browns brought in and those cocktails you talked about. We'll just party!"

He was trying to be peppy and positive for Mildred Dixon.

"I do need to ask you a question, though. It's an important one. Did Bert, by any chance, change his last name back to Vinelli? I'm getting some conflicting information on this, and I need to get that cleared up."

Mildred struggled to speak, her words coming out slower and more slurred. "That'll be so nice to see him again. My Bert and me. We're finally going to get hitched. But he's not in California . . . I know that."

She closed her eyes, then slowly lifted her tremulous right hand, which appeared frail with large, prominent veins. She placed her hand on top of his and stroked it lightly, then whispered, "My Sonny Boy. My dear Sonny Boy." She paused. "I am so very grateful to you." With that, Mildred Dixon faded back to sleep.

He shook her shoulders gently and said, "Dixon, you didn't answer my question; did Bert change his last name back to Vinelli when he enlisted in the army? Is it B-E-R-T or B-U-R-T? What do you mean he's not in California? Do you know where he's at?"

She didn't answer because she had fallen back asleep.

38

Mildred Dixon was officially classified by Dr. Jones as being in a coma-tose state. She had not woken up since Jack first arrived. She responded slowly to touch, and whenever anyone would talk to her, she would move slightly, but otherwise she was nonresponsive to any other stimuli.

Jack came to visit her often throughout the day. It was almost med-itative, he thought, to be in this room where they had so many deep conversations about her youth and his feelings. The room was quiet except for the throaty and irregular breathing sounds emerging from deep inside Mildred's sick lungs. As he looked out, there was a break in the thick clouds that permitted sunlight to sneak through the win-dow blinds, turning the dusky room to a lighter shade of gray. Despite the change in weather to unseasonable coolness, the room was made warmer by the sun. He was fearful that death would soon cast the room with a permanent silence. The gloom had a profound chill.

I gotta find him! I need to find Bert or whatever his name is! thought Jack. *If he's not in California, where the hell is he? What's his real last name? Dixon, please wake up. Help me, Dixon, and give me more information!*

39

"Code five hundred! Code five hundred! Code five hundred!" blared the overhead speakers. Suddenly, everyone's pagers went off with a loud shrill, directing them to go to room 628 on the Six North ward.

That's Mildred's room! thought Jack, and he immediately ran toward it.

Dr. Jones and Ahgri Zuri, who were down the hallway, followed and ran toward the room where there was a large gathering of nurses, doctors, and students.

Bright red blood was everywhere, on the bed, floor, Mildred's night-gown—everywhere. Mildred was pale and was still as the room became noisy and chaotic.

Where is the blood coming from? wondered Jack. He tried his best to assist those directly involved with the lifesaving activities.

Dr. Jones immediately took control of the situation and barked out orders to the nurses, other doctors, and the medical students that were close by. They soon realized the blood was coming from the rectal area. "She's bleeding out!" yelled Dr. Jones. "We need a blood trans-fusion right away! Someone put a subclavian line in! Now!" Dr. Jones listened to her lungs and heart. "Heart is feeble, and she has shallow respirations! Get some oxygen on her right now! The BP monitor doesn't look like it's functioning. Let's get a working monitor in here, STAT! Come on, people, let's move it! This lady is dying in front of our eyes, and we won't let that happen! Get rid of those blood-soaked sheets, and get her gown off. We don't want her to get hypothermic from the blood that's cooling!"

After about another hour of chaos, Dr. Jones had everything under control, and he ordered others to start dispersing. "Okay, people, we've got too many chefs in the kitchen now, so get back to your regular duties. Maizel, you and Zuri stick around to help me finish up here. Maizel, good job on that subclavian! I think we got the transfusion as quickly as we could. She should be volume expanded again. Her BP is stable, but she's still unconscious and still in a comatose state. We need to get her more stable and move her into the ICU. She's not looking too good for my comfort!"

Jack Maizel and Ahgri Zuri nodded but didn't say anything. One of the nurses asked if there was a DNR—a do-not-resuscitate—order in place for her.

"No, that concept just became popular around 1976 and we don't have that as a convention yet," said Dr. Jones. "We need to get with the times. I'll bring it up to the hospital committee on ethics, but in the meantime, it's all-out activity to try to keep our patients alive!"

40

The intensive care unit, ICU, was designed in a circular manner. The nurses' station occupied the center while each patient unit was situated in a radial pattern, much like a pie cut into triangular pieces. Each unit was called a pod and housed all necessary life support and resuscitation equipment. The occupants of each pod were constantly visible to the medical personnel and access was in real time in case of emergencies, which occurred quite often in the ICU.

The entire unit was often bathed in a cacophony of sounds that included buzzes, bells, and pumps from ventilators, intravenous fluid pumps, and various other alarm-generating equipment.

The noises produced a discordant effect upon those who worked in these units. In addition, the regularity of poor medical outcomes often resulted in frequent headaches, fatigue, and even foul moods. Regular breaks away from the room were a must for employees who worked in the unit for any length of time.

This unit truly earned the moniker of God's waiting room. Each piece of equipment helped hold on to life just a little bit longer, but the hand-holding would soon lose its grip, and the patients succumbed to their destiny of death—looming at their doorsteps.

Mildred Dixon was transferred to one of the pod units immediately after the hemorrhagic incident she suffered just two days ago that kept her in a state of unconsciousness. Her skin was a pasty pale yellow from the horrific loss of blood plus the increasing jaundice from the liver failure. This contrasted sharply with the wispy, unkempt white hair, very much noticeable under the stark, bright fluorescent lighting of the room.

A tarnished yellow notebook paper folded several times over was on the floor next to her bed. It apparently fell out of her Bible when they transferred her to the unit. It was torn and crinkled from age but obviously was important to the elderly lady.

Jack, still shook up over the events of the past two days, examined Mildred's heart and lungs, moving the necklace that she always wore as he placed his stethoscope at different locations of the lung fields. He shined a penlight into her eyes as he lifted the lids of each.

He picked up the paper and gently attempted to insert it into the Bible when a two-dollar bill, also doubled over a few times, fell out. He gently took both and slipped them into his pocket to investigate later.

Dr. Khan, the ICU attending physician, stopped by. "Rough day, huh?" he said. "Our assessment of the patient is not good, and we recommend getting hospice involved for palliative care as soon as possible. Does this patient have family members here? If not, you may want to alert them to see her. I don't believe she has much longer. Too much blood and volume loss from this episode. She has widely scattered mets from her cancer and cannot hang on too much longer. Any questions?"

"Yes, just one. I'm not clear why Dixon had the rectal bleeding. She was stable except for being in an intermittent state of consciousness for a few days. Can you explain the pathophysiology of this event?"

"Quite simple!" said Dr. Khan. "This patient has pancreatic cancer that spread to the liver, right? That means the liver is not producing any or very little of the proteins and other biochemicals that it normally does. Normally, these protein particles, as you know, are solutes that increase the osmotic pressures in the bloodstream. Thus, when the amount of solutes decline, the osmotic pressure declines, and the blood may leak out of the body. Besides, the coagulation proteins are sparse now—she is just not making them any longer, and she can't clot in the usual sense. Therefore, she bled out through her rectal area."

"Okay, that makes sense. Just one other thing, Dr. Khan. I do want to tell you that she has a longtime boyfriend who I am trying to find—long story! But what she really wants is to go home so she can die there—around familiar surroundings. She's a nurse and knows that she was diagnosed with metastatic disease and doesn't have too much longer to live. Could we at least try to do that? Just send her home, please?"

"Unfortunately and absolutely not, Maizel! She needs hospice care around the clock, and there is no way she could be alone. My understanding is that where she lives, there is limited if any hospice availability, correct? If we disconnected all the wires and lifesaving measures we are doing now, she would die right away. I would recommend she stay here, hooked up to the ventilators until she passes. Besides, it would also be a legal liability for the hospital if we simply let her go home in this terminal condition. We will just need to manage her here to the best of our abilities!"

With that, Khan left to see the next patient.

Jack, still shaken, brushed Mildred's hair back gently and tried to straighten it as he sat by her bedside, taking over the duties of a family member.

He pulled out the two-dollar bill from his pocket, unfolded it, and noticed that a large piece from the right top corner was torn. *What does that mean?*

He slipped the piece of paper out from his pocket, too, and carefully unfolded it—he could tell that it was folded and unfolded many times—and discovered it consisted of two pages of a handwritten letter, back and front. On the first page and a half of the note, in a clear and neat handwriting, the words were legible, while the words on the bottom half

of the last page were written in what looked like a child's handwriting—
the hand of someone under duress.

13 October 1943

My Dear Mildred,

I have a lot on my mind as I write this letter to you.

First, I want to tell you that I have only loved once, and that is with you. You are my TRUE LOVE! I am fulfilled and content with US—you and me! I will never want or need anyone else to love, care, and die for.

I have shared with you every detail of my past, my thoughts about the present, my hopes, dreams, and feelings for our future— with you, my dear Mildred. I cannot wait to see how we fare in our lives. The beautiful kids we will have, the dream house we will live in, and the happiness and beauty that will bestow our surroundings and even the glorious vacations we will take! We will live the happiness along with sadness.

Now for the sadness. The war is weighing heavily on my mind, heart, and soul, Mildred. I pray to God that He ends it soon. Now, would be better! Please stop it! No more destruction, no more death, and please no more erasure of beauty. War—such an ugly act that mankind has invented. For what? For what purpose do we destroy, mutilate, and kill? How do we as human beings create such rage and devastation? Why do we pillage, rape, and ruin each other, our homes, and lives? Think about the simple, everyday matters we do in life, like bask in a warm shower or lounge in a bathtub, have hot meals, and tell stories as a family. Smile, laugh, love, and enjoy life—to sleep in a nice, warm, and cozy bed.

The poor people I bomb with my airplane don't have the same luxuries! They can't. They must run, they step on dead bodies, breathe in heavy smoke, see horrors beyond imagination, and look to get away from the violence. They exude every bad emotion of humankind—they scream in horror and cry in sadness. They don't know what tomorrow will bring except certain misery and the smell of death. Why? Why, Mildred? Only an evil mind can conjure up something so hellish!

I'm sorry to tell you all this, but I need to relieve it from my mind. I live it every day, and it is taking a toll on me. Don't get me wrong, I love going up in the air and seeing the beautiful earth from high above, but it is so frightening to be shot at from below and having those small, fast, and powerful airplanes flying all around our airplane and shooting at us. Knowing that there are people who want us killed or the plane to fall from the sky is a terrifying thought.

The strange thing is, I don't even know these people, and they don't know me. Why do they want to kill me? Why do I want to kill them? Why do we, as a people, seem to always be destroying God's creation? War is such an illogical, sad, and evil event. Every time I suit up and review my mission and get on that plane, I prepare for death and realize that my odds of dying are damned high.

I don't want to leave, Mildred. I don't want to leave you and lose what might have been with us. I want to see you, hold you, and kiss you so tight and so hard. How do I reconcile with this? How do I make this go away and turn around and hold you for eternity?

I often listen to music to keep my mind off things, but it seems like every word of every lyric sends the same message. The words are "I'm missing my love" and "I'll see you soon!" You know I always . . . always and always think about you, my love. The other day, I was listening to a beautiful version of a song about how we'll see each other again. It's such a beautiful tune, Mildred. I caught myself wanting to see you now, tomorrow, and every day. When will we meet again? Soon, I hope.

There's another song I keep listening to about how I'll see you soon. In a part of the song, two lovers—like us—are so far apart, but they look at the moon at the exact same time and they can see each other. Do you remember that time on the Idlewild steamboat in Louisville, I told you that same story? So please look at the moon every chance you get, and I will, too. Maybe we'll see each other! It'll give me so much comfort to imagine we are looking into each other's eyes through the moon. Is this God's telephone for us?

Tomorrow, I will go on another mission. I cannot say where or when, but I'm already afraid. Afraid to die and to never see you again. I'm not embarrassed to tell you this! Psychologists say that being scared is a protective mechanism for human beings and other animals. It's like a danger warning sign. Well, it doesn't take a smart guy to figure out that flying a piece of metal with explosives on board while others are trying to shoot you down is not a good thing and that it makes an excellent warning sign.

It does give me comfort to be able to talk about it and share my feelings with you, my dear Mildred. Thank you!

I must go now; the commanding officer wants to see us for a briefing about tomorrow's bombing mission. I'll finish later.

For now, please know that I love you with all my heart for all time!

I'll Be Seeing You (soon)
Always,

PS: I always carry that two-dollar bill you gave me for good luck! I know that you have the corner you tore, and when we get back together, we'll tape it back up and be whole again! Also, I'm just about done with my part of our wedding band! I love you—

Jack was curious that he did not sign the letter, but he assumed it had to be a letter from Bert—the man she wanted to find before she died.

Below this letter—probably written the next day and obviously on the bombing mission. It was in bigger writing, as if written under severe duress and probably not during the most ideal situation. It was marked by brownish smeared stains and what looked like grease or oil stains.

Mil—on plane somewhere over Ger—just got hit hurts bad— maybe a while until I get wel . . . just keep look at moon—i'll be see you . . . soon

I love you foreve—
D—

Jack, guessing the note was written by Bert, but found it curious that the initial was a *D* instead of a *B* for Bert. But perhaps it was supposed to be a *B*? For obvious reasons, the man could not form letters clearly or correctly.

Jack was having difficulties holding back tears as he read the heartfelt letter twice. He imagined what it must have been like for Bert. Jack folded the heavily tarnished yellow notebook papers and carefully placed it back into Mildred's Bible. He put the two-dollar bill with the corner missing into his pocket for now, wanting to see if he could find the corner piece later among her belongings. He wanted to tape it together for her.

Mildred Dixon passed away to eternity two hours later.

41

It was the thirtieth day of September, Jack realized. He remembered Mildred Dixon quoting the grade school poem that helped people remember how many days there were in every month. *Yup, you are right, Dixon! There are thirty days in September.*

A steady rain pelted rhythmically against the black umbrellas. It was a cool and damp, end-of-September morning, which contrasted considerably with the weather just one month ago, thought Jack. The leaves were turning colors—some a brilliant orange and red while others pigmented to only a dull brown. Many had begun to fall from their mother branches and covered much of the grounds of the heavily treed cemetery.

Three men, dressed in dark clothing, stood beside one another. The tall, lanky man in the middle stood ramrod straight wearing a checkered red-and-blue blanket that was draped over his upper body. It completely covered his black suit and tie underneath. All three stood at the foot end of the rectangular cavity that was dug into the earth that morning.

The head end of the grave site was marked with a previously placed headstone that had overgrowth so thick the markings were illegible at first glance. Jack Maizel thought it peculiar that Mildred Dixon's name had not been carved into the stone yet, even though it must have been purchased quite some time ago.

The elderly minister suddenly burst out in a recital of Psalm 23—"The Lord Is My Shepard"—as he walked toward the head of the grave and stood slightly stooped, holding an open Bible. His umbrella was carefully balanced over his right shoulder as he held the heavy book with both hands and began to read another passage.

Jack Maizel and Ahgri Zuri now stood side by side, next to one end of the casket supported by wooden props. As Jack listened, he could not help thinking that it was peculiar that Mildred had already erected a monument. Certainly, he knew of couples who had bought them to prepare for the inevitable. It would help lessen the burden on their loved ones. But Mildred had no one else, and she hadn't been sick that long. Why would she have purchased a headstone already? It was clearly a double monument. Besides it looked as if she bought it quite some time ago. Did she think her death would come at an early age?

As the minister read from the Bible, Ahgri slipped an envelope into his friend's hands and whispered, "I forgot to give this to you. Miss Mildred said to tell you not to open it until after the services were over." He snickered slightly. "Strict orders, my friend!" he said in a low voice. "She also wanted you to have this." He handed him a necklace. "Miss Mildred told me that when she died, she wanted me to take the necklace off her and give it to you. It has deep meaning. *Kushikiliwa kwa kina!*"

Jack did not acknowledge him. He simply nodded slightly and placed the envelope into his inner coat pocket. He looked at the necklace for a few seconds, put it in his pants pocket, and held back tears.

As the service proceeded, Jack's mind began to wander again. His heart was heavy with sorrow, and his soul was tired. How his life had turned around in such a short period of time—so full of significant events and deep conversations. It took only thirty days to turn his despised life to a life with true purpose, want, and service.

"Thirty days hath September," Dixon had declared when she first met him. She even recited the poem for him. And now this. How ironic that it would become her last month on this earth. He had grown to care for her but also knew that he could never help defeat the cancer that ravaged her body. The only way he knew how to help her was to find her past love. He failed to find him in time, but he found himself.

A real miracle. The entire ordeal changed him into a better person, he was convinced. *I'm grateful to her for inspiring and trusting me to find her Bert,* he thought. It still bothered him that he didn't know whether the man's name was Bert or Burt or if his last name was Vines or Vinelli. *But, caring felt so good!* he thought. *Why didn't I ever experience this after Ajax died? How could I have let myself turn so hateful? Who was this woman that came into my life from nowhere?*

He thought about how she lectured him on passion and purpose. How Ahgri brought wisdom to his life. Jack felt that he was finally on the right course to become a better man with the only two people who really cared about him. His life's compass was now facing the right way.

He also thought about the events at the Boy Scout camp that changed his life. He knew then that his destiny was to be the doctor who his parents wanted him to be. Only now, it was what he wanted. He was beginning to understand a different view of life. No more rich people parties. No more doing what others told him to do. Not even his parents! He was going to do what was right for him, and he was going to lead with his heart.

When the service was completed, the minister left, and Ahgri said he had commitments and needed to get back to the hospital. Jack thanked them and gave Ahgri a hug.

As he watched the gravediggers toss the wet dirt onto the coffin, now lying deep within the grave, a sudden urge to clean some of the overgrowth from the headstone gripped him. When he reached to remove some of the weeds from the stone, he didn't bother to roll up his suit sleeve, not caring whether it would get soiled or not. The rain had loosened the dirt, and the vegetation was easier to clear than he thought. He didn't care whether this would dirty his hands or clothing. He just wiped them off on his expensive full-length greatcoat. *Ms. Dixon is worth that much.*

As Jack pulled the weeds, he noticed some markings on the headstone. As he continued to brush the caked-on dirt and growth from the granite monument, an engraved name and numbers appeared on the right side. It was clear that the headstone was made for a couple. The left side, where Ms. Dixon's casket was placed, appeared blank.

The engraving was unclear at first, but suddenly Jack jolted backward while letting out an involuntary shriek! Bewildered, he shook his head back and forth and gasped at what he just saw. He inhaled deeply until his chest tightened and he could no longer inhale. Suddenly frightened, he pulled back; his body felt completely drained, and the blood seemed to leave his face. It was as if he had seen an apparition.

Jack wiped his eyes from the rain. But as plain as the day, the name Delbert Paul Vines was etched into the stone, staring back at him. The inscription dates—born June 5, 1917, died October 14, 1943—verified the lifetime of this individual. In decorative characters, an engraving underneath the dates completed the epitaph:

> My Precious Soulmate
> Our Love will live in my memory and heart always,
> and "We'll Meet Again" to part no more.
>
> Always,
>
> Mildred

Jack Maizel's emotions overflowed. He was having difficulty catching his breath. *So, Bert is short for Delbert and his name was Vines, not Vinelli,* thought Jack. She had known all along that Delbert, or, as she called him, Bert, had died in the war! *How dare she make me go on a wild goose chase all over Kentucky, desperately looking for this man. How could she have lied to me?*

Suddenly, he hated her. No, he despised her.

Jack did not know what to do, so he sprinted to his car that was parked at the edge of the road, leaving his umbrella on the ground by the grave. He scooted into the driver's side of the car, trying to catch his breath. His heart was beating fast, and his skin was clammy from both perspiration and rain. His mind swirled frantically, trying to make sense of what he just saw and reliving the past thirty days.

What did this woman do to me? Why? He thought of how he stood up for her and how he befriended her. He trusted and believed what she had told him. *They were all lies*, he concluded. *Just lies—a big fat joke on me! She lied to get back at me for how I first treated her.*

He continued to stare out the window for a long while afterward, thinking about how he'd been had. But he didn't bother to turn the wipers on—no desire to look out into the world just yet.

Suddenly, feeling claustrophobic, he loosened his tie and started to take his greatcoat and jacket off. A slight stiffness and a crumpling noise came from the left inside coat pocket. Reaching inside, he recalled his friend handing him the envelope during the service.

He tore it open and pulled out the contents—a piece of triangular paper fell out. He was shocked and instantly recognized it as the corner piece of US currency. *Probably from that two-dollar bill I found in the folded yellow paper.*

He then carefully unfolded the faintly scented sheets of letter paper from the rest of the envelope. His tense face calmed slightly as he started to read:

September 10, 1982

Dear Sonny Boy:

Right about now, you are probably confused and maybe a little angry with me. As you can see by the date of this letter, I'm still "alive and kick'n'," as you often told me.

But I do know that I'm going to die—and I know it'll be soon. You haven't told me yet, and I'm not sure that you will, but sometimes I can hear all you doctors talk about me outside my door. I don't understand everything you say—I'm not a cancer nurse, remember?—but I know that it's clear that I won't be around too much longer. I don't feel well and know there's something bad happening to me.

Now, as my favorite radio newsman would say, THE REST OF THE STORY about Delbert and me, and why I did what I did to you. Some of the story you know already, but I'll go over it again, so it'll make more sense to you.

First, so that we are clear on the names. My love's real name was Delbert. Yes, I called him Bert every once in a while, but he was really Delbert. His real last name was originally Vinelli, but his family Americanized it to Vines like so many Italian Americans did when they first arrived on our shores. His name was always Vines. I gave you the Bert name to throw you off a bit on purpose. You never asked how it was spelled or if it was short for something. That's okay. You played my game. I confused you on purpose.

When I first met my dear Delbert, I fell in love so hard, I could barely think straight. He was my first love, you know. And as fate would have it—my one and only.

Funny, I wasn't even looking for a man those days. Far from it, Sonny Boy. He was a good-looking man but had the cutest boyish mannerisms. He reminded me of a Sonny Boy in my mind—in a good way. So, when I met you, I thought you looked just like a little boy, too—but a bad one! Very mischievous. It fit you just right! I knew you didn't like to be called that so that's why I kept using it. It annoyed you, I know, but just like you did to me, calling me by my last name, Dixon, as if I was in some army or prison, irked me, too. I didn't like it. So, I guess we just aggravated the heck out of each other.

Just a little more about Delbert so you know him, too. His voice was so soft and unassuming, yet he had this powerful effect on me. I was so intensely attracted to this lovely man. As I write this to you, I still get butterflies when I think of that first encounter.

Anyway, romance blossomed before the blink of an eye. We met, fell in love, and planned our futures together within a couple of weeks. You see, back then, things had to be done in a hurry because of the war and all.

I was convinced he would never die because I knew God had other plans for him. You see, Delbert was an extremely bright young man. His dream was that once he got back, he would become an architect. I told you that he wanted to build things—beautiful things. He certainly had the hands and mind to do it. They were works of art—beautiful—so gentle and graceful.

We met the morning he had to leave. His friend Lieutenant Van Miller set it up for us. Yes, I'm not ashamed to say that we made beautiful love on a humongous B-17 airplane. A weapon of destruction, but we made love in it. Isn't that ironic?

Afterward, I gave him the two-dollar bill with the corner ripped off it, and he gave me the necklace I'm giving you. Delbert made the ring that's on it out of a 1942 nickel. It was supposed to be my wedding band, and he was making another one for himself. When he got home, we were going to wear them as our testament of marriage. Maybe you can complete our story by using it as your own wedding band someday. That would make our spirits happy!

Then, suddenly he was gone; we were no longer "us." We were no longer together as we had dreamed. The man I loved suddenly vanished. Poof! Just like that, he disappeared into thin air! And as bad luck or fate would have it, he never came back.

My Delbert never came back to me—alive that is. So, you see, I did see him again, like I told you, but not alive, sadly. When they shipped his body back for burial, he had left explicit instructions for me to take care of his remains—I kept a low profile about the burial since we weren't married, and it caused quite a rift with his relatives in California. After all, who was I to anyone else, especially to his family? Back then, it was considered a bit illicit if men and women were too intimate and, God forbid, if sex happened! You know everyone did it anyway. Everyone has done it since the beginning of time. How do people think they got here? So, you see, I didn't lie to you about that part. I did see my Delbert here in Kentucky!

I bought a double headstone and bought two plots side by side because I knew that when I died, I wanted to be physically next to him. I already knew that I'd spend eternity with him and my God in heaven, and that's where our marriage would finally be celebrated. I would marry him in heaven with God as my witness! And you know something? I can hardly wait!

So, you're probably asking yourself what does this have to do with me? When I first met you, Sonny Boy, I hated you. You were arrogant and mean and had no compassion at all. Yes, you were like a mean, rotten rascal of a boy, so full of yourself—a real Sonny Boy in my opinion. Then after I got to know you a bit better and studied those hands of yours—just like Delbert's—you started to remind me of him. My Delbert was a kind man with a good heart, but sometimes he could get irascible too—just like a naughty boy. But that was actually fun to see because he was a determined man, and he usually got his way.

After I learned more about you from your friend, Ahgri—what a fine human being he is—I knew you needed help. You lived a life of leisure with no hardships or difficulties. You were living a false life! Very dysfunctional and not real! No wonder you had become mean and uncaring. And your poor horse, Ajax. I'm sorry about that episode of your life.

But I knew you had a good heart, and I wanted to bring that out in you. I wanted you to learn to care about something or someone. I wanted you to care about me! I somehow knew that if I did what I did to you—go looking for my man who did not exist—it would give you some difficulties but you would learn a lesson and understand yourself better. Qualities that would help you become a great doctor and help you with your personal life. You would have a purpose. I hope I was right. Yes, I did use a bit of psychology on you—but remember, I'm a psyche nurse!

I hope that this letter cleared up some things for you and gives you some peace. By the way, the corner of a two-dollar bill is enclosed. I hope you find the other part of the bill that Delbert had. If you do, please put the two pieces together so that Delbert and I can be whole again. Then keep it in a special place for us.

I sincerely hope that you will one day be consumed with the love and contentment Bert and I had. I hope that we built a bridge for you. One that would span the rest of your life. I want you to be fulfilled, Sonny Boy. It will be a good life for you.

So, thank you, Dr. Jack Maizel, for helping me during the last days of my life. You will be a fine doctor as long as you care about

people, have a deep sense of compassion, and, most of all, have a
strong sense of purpose.
    Sincerely and best wishes for a happy and purposeful life!

Always, my dear Sonny Boy!

Mildred

Tears fell unashamedly from Jack's eyes. He could not stop. Outside, the pounding of the rain increased in frequency and force. It slammed against the metal roof of the automobile, making loud hollow sounds inside. Deafening, in fact. It was as if the heavens had opened and were crying with him. He sat for a while longer, feeling numb.

His emotions simmered down, and exhaustion now consumed him. The emotional roller coaster overwhelmed him as he sat—almost slumped in the driver's seat. The rain had slowed down to almost a halt, allowing him to view his surroundings more clearly. Rolling down the driver's side window partway, he took a deep breath and glanced upward toward the sky. He noticed that the clouds were breaking up as he caught a glimpse of bright blue patches amid the heavy rain clouds. The sun made an occasional grand entrance as the clouds rapidly rolled by. A faint smile came across his face as he wiped away the last of his tears.

He reached for the keys, then inserted one into the ignition and gave it a quick twist. The engine immediately responded with a soft purr. Jack rolled down the window, this time all the way, feeling the refreshed but still cool, damp air against his face and scalp. Closing his eyes, he took another deep breath. He glanced one final time to where Mildred Dixon had just been buried. With a smile of gratitude, he whispered, "Thank you, Dixon."

Putting the car into gear and in motion, he watched the beads of rain that had rested on the windshield roll toward the edges of the frame. Without having to turn on the wipers, he headed slowly away in the direction of the cemetery gates. He could now see out the window unhindered, but more importantly, his life's destiny had now become clear. He could thank Mildred Dixon for that.

42

Mountain Clinic, located at one end of the small shopping plaza, was the dominant business on this strip of stores. While most of the shopping center appeared old and rundown, the medical office sported a simple brick façade that had a large window. Located next to a country-style door, it was a pleasing frontage when compared with the rest of the businesses.

A sign located next to the door declared—

Aligri Zuri, MD, FAAFP, Family Practice

Jack Maizel, MD, FAAFP, Family Practice

William Jones, MD, PhD, ABIM Consulting Physician

Medical Doctors for Your Entire Family

Office Hours 8 a.m.–6:00 p.m. Monday through Friday

Saturday 9 a.m.–12 p.m.

Closed on Sundays

Appointments & Walk-Ins are always welcome

A few children romped around the waiting area as if they were at a school playground or a family picnic. Others slumbered against their mothers' laps. Still others, especially the sick kids, clutched tightly against their moms' soft bosoms, resting their heads and listening to the soothing heartbeats, not in the least interested in play or conversation.

The elderly patients, for the most part, sat properly, not complaining about the noise level but almost ignoring it as they busily exchanged gossip with one another.

While the business of the clinic created a certain noise level that sounded like a drone of bees, any interruption—such as the calling of a name or a new patient entering through the front door—would instantly quiet the room, just for a moment, before it resumed its clamor.

Just then, a young woman with an infant in her arms opened the front entrance door and proceeded to the receptionist's desk. Everyone stopped what they were doing for a few seconds to eye the newcomer but immediately resumed their conversations.

The front desk receptionist said, "Hi, Mary Jane, how's that new baby of yours?"

"She kept me up all night a cry'n' and a spittin' up. I just don't know what's wrong with her. I s'pose that's why I'm here. I need to see the doctor."

"Well, you know you're considered a walk-in, so you may have to wait a tad longer. If you can do that, I'll squeeze you in. Now, who do you want to see, Dr. Maizel or Dr. Zuri?"

"Don't make no difference to me. My other kids love them both, so give me whoever is freed up the soonest."

The receptionist looked at the schedule book and replied, "Looks like Dr. Zuri might be your best bet. Go ahead and have a seat. I'll call you when he's ready for you."

Behind the receptionist area, it was as busy and chaotic as the waiting area. There were six clinical exam rooms and a larger room for procedures. Two for each of the three doctors.

Jack and Ahgri started their medical practice immediately after they finished a family practice residency training. Dr. Jones joined them when he retired from the university to give him something to do and to help with the more complicated cases his two former favorite students had. The three became best of friends, especially when Jack invited him to a few of his family's parties.

*   *   *

"Hey, Jack, you have a direct phone call in my office," yelled Ahgri. "Want me to transfer it to your office or take it on my phone?"

Jack Maizel was cradling an infant in one arm and carrying a large diaper bag in the other while he accompanied a mother who was pushing a stroller and managing two tots with her free hands. He had a wide grin and seemed happy.

"Tell whoever it is I'll call back in a few minutes," said Jack. "Mrs. Lovett here has her hands full, and I'm just helping her out to the car. I'll be right back."

As Ahgri mused at the spectacle before him, he said, "You know, Jack, you look extremely comfortable and confident with children around you . . . and especially holding the diaper bags. Would you just once and for all find a good woman, have your own children, and live a happy life? After all, you look good. You lost weight, cleaned up, and are in shape now. Of course, many thanks to me for taking you up these Appalachian Mountains every week to climb! You may finally be able to attract a woman or two to be your wife!" He paused. "Oh, by the way, the telephone call is from Dr. John Tenneson in Lexington," Ahgri said, with half his body inside his office and half out. "You know Dr. God himself? The man you worship!"

"Oh. What's he want?" Jack asked.

"He states something to the effect of wanting you to reconsider his many offers about partnership. He appears to desperately want you to work with him.

"You do know, my friend, that this would require you to go back into a surgical residency program. Another three to five years more at least. He does not have your best interest, Jack. He is one of those very malevolent insects. An insect like him is essentially a parasite."

Jack Maizel stared at his colleague for a second, then looked at the tired and overwhelmed mother who tried to control her two restless boys. He felt good with his life right now.

Taking a quick assessment of his life—he indeed had lost weight and had been helping Ahgri guide climbing expeditions up some of the local mountains on weekends. No more haunting dreams or thoughts about Ajax, and he absolutely liked his life.

Jack even bought a few acres at the base of some Appalachian foothill mountains and built a small ranch with two horses.

His parents eventually gave in to Jack, realizing they'd never make him do what they wanted and agreed to convert some of their eight-hundred-acre Thoroughbred racehorse farm into a horse sanctuary that he could run and operate. Finally, Dr. Jack Maizel knew he wanted to have his own family, too. But would he ever find the right woman? Would he ever be able to emulate Mildred and Bert's successful romance? That would be how he would gauge any relationship.

A wide smile came over his face, and he looked back at his friend with a chuckle. "Zuri, tell that no-good insect of a man that Dr. Jack Maizel has gone home and for him to go fly a kite and drift away somewhere far with it. Tell him not to be a pest and not to bug me anymore! Oh, and make sure you tell him to have a good day and that he should always watch out for the beneficial insects around him. They will surely devour him! Then you can hang up on him!"

Ahgri nodded and smiled. "You have come a long way since medical school, my friend, Jack Maizel. Ever since you started taking regular baths and grooming properly, you appear to the public with distinction as a fine citizen should. I am very proud of who you have become, my friend!" He chuckled. "Some ladies may even say you have a certain *je ne sais quoi*! But I will tell you . . . I shall terribly miss those baseball caps that leave such incredible artistic impressions and designs on your forehead!"

With that, he shut the door and a loud howling laughter soon emanated through the walls.

* * *

Jack Maizel quickly glanced at the next patient's chart. The chief complaint read, "Twenty-eight-year-old single female with good general health but recently was bucked off a horse and now experiencing back pains. Wants to be checked out for it."

Jack smiled and knocked lightly as he walked into the next exam room. The young doctor, taken aback by the patient's incredibly beautiful smile and her exuberance, extended his hand. *Quite striking*, he thought.

"Hi, I'm Dr. Maizel, a family doctor. Please call me Jack!"

"Hello, Jack the Doctor!" the patient cheerily replied.

With a pleasant smile, she introduced herself. "I'm Mildred Rose. Most people call me by my last name—Rose! I would love it if you would just call me Rose, too!"

Jack Maizel paused for a second. He grinned widely. "Hi, Rose! So, you got bucked off a horse?"

"Yes, I just moved here last December, and a teacher colleague of mine knew of this horse ranch down the road from the school where we teach. She said we could get free riding lessons the first two times out. Two free ones, then we have to pay for at least five more times. Maybe a gimmick, but I wanted to ride again. I never rode horses, only ponies when I was a little girl. I had a pony named Achilles, back in Ohio. I loved riding. Most of the time, I rode until it got dark. I just loved it. I think I tired him out most every day, but he was my love! My best friend! I never tried horseback riding—they're just big ponies, right? So, I tried it, but then this happened!"

She was simply beautiful, and Jack could not help but be mesmerized by her. Everything about her was perfect! Incredible beauty in her face, lovely hair, great personality—she even smelled good.

"Long story short," continued Rose, "we went riding last week, and as soon as I got on him, he kicked both hind limbs out and I got thrown! It was funny at first, but, a day or so later I started hurting all over, especially my lower back area. So, I'm here to just get myself checked to make sure I didn't break anything!"

Jack said, "I'll look you over, but do you know the most important part of horse-related injuries?"

"No, tell me, Jack the Doctor!"

She was a feisty thing, Jack gathered, but spirited in a joyful way. She reminded him of his mother's spunk but in a much more toned manner and Mildred Dixon's kind demeanor. He liked her!

"You need to be able to ride a horse properly, and to do that, you need to have a good teacher. I am a good one, and I will teach you how to ride if you are willing to let me!"

Rose, excited, said, "Oh! I am game for that! So, you're a doctor for horse riding, too? Did you learn how to ride in medical school, Jack the Doctor?"

"You could say that! By the way, did you say your pony's name was Achilles?"

Rose looked at him a bit puzzled. "Yes, but does that have anything to do with my aches and pain?"

Jack, smiling incredulously, said, "Did you know that Achilles and Ajax were cousins?"

Rose looked upward, as if to think back. "My college major was English lit, but secretly, I loved reading Greek mythology on the side, so, yes, I do know they were cousins, but Achilles was killed by an arrow to his heel—shot by Paris. And poor Ajax was so forlorn about his cousin's death that later he killed himself in a moment of insanity when he didn't have access to Achilles's armor. He wanted the armor because it would have made him feel closer to his beloved cousin!"

Jack clapped. "You are brilliant, Ms. Rose! You are correct!"

Wow, smart, beautiful, and fun. I found my soulmate! the young doctor mused.

Rose, perplexed, smiled and said, "Look, Jack the Doctor, I am confused. I still don't know why a doctor is quizzing me about Greek mythology when I am here about getting checked out for a possible injury from a horse. Am I missing something?" She put her hand under her chin and looked contemplative. "Wait! Please tell me you are not one of those quack doctors."

Jack, still smiling, said, "No, not that I last checked. But please, do me a favor, Rose, I want you to call me—"

"Call you Jack the Doctor? You already told me!" she interrupted playfully.

He crossed his arms in front of his chest and said, "Nope!" He was still smiling from ear to ear and feeling a bit giddy. "I would be honored if you would call me . . . Sonny Boy!"

AFTERWORD

Forty years have passed since I roamed the hallways of my medical alma mater. The theater of my mind has recorded thousands of hours spent in lecture and study halls, musty-smelling books in basement libraries, bright lights of surgical suites, cacophony of sounds in emergency rooms, the starkness of intensive care units, and, more importantly, the deeply ingrained emotional experiences of anxiety, dread, and sadness!

Joyful events balanced those unwanted ones to help make my chosen vocation as a pediatrician tolerable and fulfilling. Passing tough exams, successfully completing a medical procedure for the first time, hearing the cries of a newborn baby, seeing smiles on new mothers, watching children laugh, and witnessing those who successfully beat the odds against death made being a doctor a wholesome and worthy profession. The richness of a medical career is dominated by our interactions with those we help and, in some cases, even those we help pass on to death. They are the ones who teach us to listen, to be compassionate, and to empathize.

I was schooled in the science of medicine, but I learned the art of listening, compassion, and empathy from my patients. For me, one such patient was Dixon. Yes, there was a Miss Dixon, but that was not her real name. Her memory and influence are forever etched in my mind and soul. She and so many other patients before and after her are the reasons I became a better doctor.

Much like a diving board at a swimming pool, medical school was a diving-off point into the many pools of patients I would come across and learn from. There was so much more to learn about being a doctor than one could get from sitting in classrooms, memorizing the Krebs cycle or gluconeogenesis!

As in the book, the real Miss Dixon was a kind soul who helped me become a better person.

She could see that I was green and quite awkward. So, I think she was easy on me. The one thing I do remember quite well was how much she wanted to go home. I was told by my attending physicians, at the time, that we simply could not let her leave until she became more stable and had hospice support at home or obtained palliative care at a local hospital near her home. Neither was to happen.

My memory of Miss Dixon and many others like her compelled me to write this work of fiction, primarily to share a message with others. A message of hope, kindness, forgiveness, and redemption. How we use our experiential knowledge and wisdom to help others through the journey of life, much like Dixon did for Sonny Boy.

Certainly, to understand that the most important lessons about life do not come from books or the classroom but from our human interactions and relationships with those we encounter every day. This is what makes life such a wonderful experience!

ACKNOWLEDGMENTS

I am grateful for so many people who have helped make my dream to publish a fiction book a reality. From my incredible home family, who provides me with everyday love, stability, and peace in my life, to my work family, who gives me everyday challenges and sometimes more excitement than I need or want, to my dear friends, who offer me other joys of life—they have all been vital to what makes me, me and what made this book possible!

I am incredibly thankful for Greenleaf Publishing and the amazing editors who helped transform this novel from a somewhat disjointed project to one that makes sense and that I think is now a pretty good story.

Finally, I want to thank my wife, Kathy, who always supported me in this endeavor despite my lack of expertise in the book-writing business! She believed in me and is my "readability editor."

ABOUT THE AUTHOR

RONALD DWINNELLS lives in Poland, Ohio, with his family. His hobbies and activities include traveling, mountain climbing, running road races, and other rigorous physical activities.

He is the author of the Axiom gold medal–winning leadership book *Don't Pick Up All the Dog Hairs*.

www.ingramcontent.com/pod-product-compliance
Lightning Source LLC
Chambersburg PA
CBHW020140120726
47903CB00007B/2342